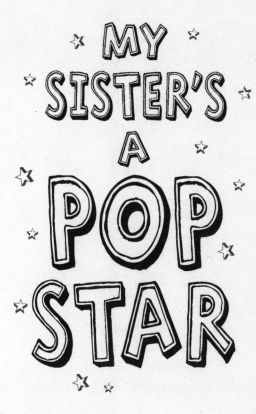

MY SISTER'S A POP STAR

Kimberly Greene

USBORNE

This book is dedicated to the three most special men in my life:
Dad, you are my role model for living a classy, fun,
and meaningful life.
Todd, you are the love of my life.
Jacob, you are the coolest stinky boy in the whole wide world.

I love you three gentlemen more than a bathtub
full of mint chocolate ice cream with whipped cream and
sprinkles on the hottest day of the year!

This edition first published in the UK in 2010 by Usborne Publishing Ltd.,
Usborne House, 83-85 Saffron Hill, London EC1N 8RT, England.
www.usborne.com

First published in 2006. Copyright © Kimberly Greene, 2006.

The right of Kimberly Greene to be identified as the author
of this work has been asserted by her in accordance with the
Copyright, Designs and Patents Act, 1988.

Cover illustration by Rui Ricardo for folioart.co.uk.

The name Usborne and the devices ♀ ⊕ are Trade Marks of
Usborne Publishing Ltd.

A CIP catalogue record for this book is available from
the British Library.

UK ISBN 9781409516507 First published in America in 2010. AE
American ISBN 9780794528997

JFMAMJJAS ND/10 01435/1   Printed in Yeovil, Somerset, UK.

CHAPTER 1

Click click click, clack clack click.

Sam's fingers were flying around the old laptop keyboard. She was way too focused on her writing to hear her mom yelling at her from the other side of the apartment. After the third "Samantha" (each one a little louder and more intense), Rose pounded forcefully on her daughter's purple bedroom door.

Sam was so jolted that she flew out of her chair. She landed on a pile of T-shirts she had yet to put into the moving box with the words "Sam's Stuff! Important Clothing – Don't Even Think About Touching" written in big red letters.

"What? What?" she yelled out.

Rose opened the door and popped her head in. "I said we have to leave for the concert in exactly fifteen minutes. Honestly, Sam, when you're at that computer, it's like nothing else exists."

Sam, having heard this many times before, rolled her eyes. "I got it, Mom. Fifteen minutes. I'll be ready."

Rose leaned in a little more. "I'm not kidding, Little Bit. Finish your blagging and get ready to go."

Rose turned and closed the door without seeing Sam's face scrunch up in annoyance.

"It's called a 'blog', Mom!" she yelled out. "A blog! I'm a blogger! I do blogging! Blog, not blag, *blog*!"

There was no response, only the clicking of Rose's heels on the wood floor as she hurried off. Sam mumbled to herself, "And now that I'm twelve, everybody needs to recognize that I'm almost a teenager and stop calling me 'Little Bit'."

Sam sighed. Lately, it felt as though nobody had time for her. She was used to being ignored and overlooked by lots of people, like Mr. Wattabee, the grumpy manager of the stables where she worked, or

Inga, the snotty little sister of Sam's best friend Olga, but the lack of attention from her mom and her sister had really become a super sore spot for Sam over the past weeks. Oh, well. She had to finish tonight's blog before leaving for the big show. Sam jumped back into her chair, cracked her knuckles, and got back to her thoughts.

This has to be the most exciting night of my entire twelve-year-old life! Danni's tour is finally ending, and it's our last night here in the apartment! I'm excited about moving, but I'm also kind of sad

Sam froze. She thought for a moment, came up with a better word, deleted "sad," and resumed typing.

melancholy, I'm very melancholy to be leaving this place.

Sam stopped typing. She took a massive slurp of orange cream soda from the bottle on her desk. As she looked up at a photo of herself and her big sister Danni,

Sam let out a little burp. She giggled in embarrassment, until she remembered she was alone in her room; no sense being embarrassed when there's nobody around to laugh at it. She returned to her typing.

This will be a short blog entry 'cause I have to get ready for Danni's concert, her last one! I'm so happy that

Sam stopped again; since anyone anywhere with access to the internet could read her web-log, she always had to use the most interesting words. She thought, deleted the word "happy," and resumed typing.

ecstatic that my big sister is finally coming home! One year may not sound like a big whoop, but it feels like forever. I've missed having Danni around. I know that it's totally not cool to say, but it officially stunk not having her home. At first it was fun getting letters from all the different places she visited, but the last couple of months she's been too busy and I've only gotten one stinky postcard. And I can't even remember the

last time Danni called just to talk to me. Who knew I would actually miss her snoring and her making fun of me? Anyway, starting tomorrow, we get our normal life back; no more tours or TV shows (after that stupid interview thing later tonight), no more Mom flying off to make sure Danni is doing her schoolwork, just our little family, and our amazing new home! I borrowed Olga's cell phone (remember Olga — my best friend — I've blogged about her before) because her phone takes way better pics than mine. So, my next blog entry will have a bunch of cool photos of the new house, my HUGE new room, and me and Danni.

Sam looked up again at the photo taped to the top of her laptop. She smiled as she remembered her and Danni posing in front of the cruddy old tour bus with that ugly yellow banner that read *"Danni Devine's Malls Across America Tour."* Hard to believe that had been a whole year ago. Sam took another sloppy slurp of soda and let out a bigger burp. She thought about how completely not normal it was to have her sister suddenly be famous. She began typing again.

Robert (Danni's agent, I've blogged about him before) keeps snidely telling me I have no idea how popular my sister has become, and not just here in the United States, but all over the world! I can't imagine folks in Canada or Mexico or China talking about Danni. I never realized how freaky it would be to have everyone on Planet Earth know my sister. Seriously, it seems like everybody knows WHO she is, but they don't know HER, the everyday, nail-chewing, bulldozer-snoring person.

Sam smiled at her witty writing, but suddenly a flash of thought hit her hard. She bit her lip and scrunched up her forehead the way she always did when she was worried about something. She began typing again very slowly.

I wonder if I should erase everything I've written here over the past year. Maybe all the personal stuff I've shared on this blog is going to cause trouble. This is a very strange situation. Before Danni was famous, I had no problem putting anything in my blog because it was just another online journal by just another nobody. Don't get me wrong, I know that I'm still just another nobody, but now that my sister isn't, is it bad to have so much stuff about us (me, Mom, and Danni...and Robert) open for the whole world to read? Of course, I'm making a pretty big, fat assumption that people are actually reading all this. For all I know the only person who's ever seen this has been Olga (Hi Olga!).

Sam heard Rose's heels clicking down the hall, coming toward her room again. She couldn't go now, not when she was in the middle of such an important blog entry. Sam ran to her bedroom door and stuck her head out into the hall.

"I'm exactly ten-point-two minutes away from being ready to go, Mom!"

Rose opened her mouth to respond, but Sam had already slipped back inside her room and closed the door.

Sam leaned against her door with both hands covering her mouth. If Rose heard her giggling, she'd be busted and forced to leave immediately.

Rose yelled back, "Sounds good. Don't forget your hat and jacket," and clicked back to the other end of the apartment.

Sam leaped back into her chair, focused on the computer screen, and frantically looked for the button that would let her search the list of all her old blog entries. She found it, clicked it, and a huge list of dates appeared on the screen. As she scrolled through the long list, Sam gave herself a mental pat on the back for using such entertaining titles for her entries. She smiled at some of her wittier writing, "*Somebody Please Tell Me I Was Adopted*," "*My Family is Nuttier Than a Snickers Bar*," and her favorite, "*I Vote Robert Ruebens off My Island*."

Sam drew in a sharp breath as she spied one of her earliest entries, entitled, "*The Facts of My Life*." She gritted her teeth as she remembered writing a lot of personal stuff in that particular blog. Her hand trembled as she reached out to click on that link.

The page popped up and the very first line made

Sam cringe. *Oh, man, I'd forgotten I wrote that*, she thought as she read her entry from a long time ago.

Sam Devine's Blog

Entry #2: The Facts of My Life

After having a very frustrating argument with my sister last night (not even worth mentioning...but she was wrong!), I hunkered down and reread one of my favorite books (*The Diary of Anne Frank*). It got me thinking that my blog might not be very interesting because I haven't told you anything about me, and it's hard to be interested in a story when you don't know the main characters, so this might be a long blog, but it should be a particularly memorable one!

I am Sam, Sam I am (LOL). Seriously, my name is Samantha Sue Devine. I love to read and I love to write. Someday I will be a great author, but for now I'm happy to practice writing by keeping this online journal. In this blog, I plan to write about my life, my dreams, and (at least for the near future) how much I wish Robert Ruebens would get a clue and quit being so evil to me (more about that later).

I love horses and plan to also be a famous equestrian. My family nicknamed me Little Bit (a name I used to love but now I'm thinking is way too "little kid") because I used to run around the house pretending to be a pony. I've been working my whole life (okay, since I was eight) at the SuAn Stables, over in the fancy part of town. Mucking out stalls is pretty gross, but each wheelbarrow of horse poop I remove gets me a whole hour of riding time. For a kid with no money, that's been a great set-up.

But I'm not a kid with no money anymore. This is where I need to introduce you to the rest of my family, my mom Rose and my big sister Danni.

My mom is beautiful. Sometimes it's hard to believe that she's so old (she's, like, thirty-seven) because she looks so young and wears clothes you'd never expect somebody's mom to wear. I don't look a thing like her. Mom has shiny dark hair; I have average brown hair. Mom has blue eyes; I have green eyes. Mom adores the color pink; I despise it; I love purple. Mom is very petite and graceful; I'm always tripping over my own two feet. Mom tells me all the time how much I look like my dad, but he died a long time ago, so I can only try to find the resemblance through a bunch of old pictures.

Mom grew up winning all the beauty pageants her mother entered her in, and there were a lot of pageants! In fact, Mom was supposed to be in the Miss America contest, but she ran off and got married instead. This is why I've never met my grandparents; they weren't too happy about my mom "throwing her life away," so they disowned her. Mom didn't care, she was really happy being married to Mr. Daniel Devine. He was a soldier, so he and Mom got to go and live in Guam (it's a tropical island that's owned by the United States — but since it's only a territory, the people who live there can't vote for president!). That's where Danni was born.

My big sister Danni (Danielle Ann) was a pretty, blue-eyed, bald, baby girl who grew up to be a beautiful, blue-eyed, blonde kid (she did eventually get some hair). Today, my sister is a wicked gorgeous sixteen-year-old! She's the girl other girls seem to want to be...at least, that's the way it looks from my perspective. Danni isn't brain-surgeon smart, but she's not dumb, either. She just has a tough time thinking things through and making decisions for herself. I've never understood that. If somebody tells me something, I don't immediately accept it; I take a minute to consider if it makes sense. Danni pretty much believes whatever you tell her. I worry that if she does become famous, this will make it easy for people to take advantage of her.

Anyway, back to my life story. So my mom is living in Guam with my dad and sister, when she finds out she's going to have another baby (me).

This is where the story gets sad.

My dad told my mom that she should make up with her parents, so he bought a ticket for her and Danni to fly back to the U.S. mainland to see my grandparents. He took Mom and Danni to the airport and kissed them goodbye. That was the last time they saw him. He died in a car crash that night. Mom got the news when her plane landed. She says she sat down in the middle of the airport, hugged Danni, and cried for about two hours.

After she stopped crying, Mom decided she wasn't going to run home and let her parents rule her life again. She opted to stay on at the local army base until I was born, but she had no idea what she would do next.

See, my mom had graduated high school, but she hadn't gone to college. She could ride a motorcycle (that was how she and my dad met) and she could look pretty, but neither of those

things could lead to a well-paid job. Mom decided that, once I was born, she would become a model – not one of those skinny, fake-looking models strutting down a runway, but the smiling mom model you see in laundry detergent ads.

So I grew up on that army base. Mom got a job in the daycare center there, so we got to live in one of those cute little base houses. Between her widow's pension, her daycare salary, and the little extra she brought in with those "smiling mom" modeling jobs, Mom made sure that me and Danni grew up never knowing how tough things really were, money-wise, I mean.

Danni was always bugging Mom to let her go on one of her modeling shoots, but Mom didn't think it was a good place for a kid to be hanging out. Finally, when Danni was ten, Mom caved in and took her to her next modeling gig. The photographer took one look at Danni, with her big blue eyes and long blonde hair, and demanded that she be in the pictures, too. Mom protested, but Danni made it clear that she wanted to do it, and the photos were really amazing!

Danni began to get her own modeling jobs and made enough money to enter a small beauty pageant. Mom was none too pleased with this, but she figured that one good loss would end Danni's fascination with the whole pageant thing. Besides, Mom had always told us that "you don't know if you don't try," so she wasn't in a position to tell Danni not to try.

And wouldn't you know, but Danni wins that pageant! Along with a trophy and a tiara, Danni received a check for five hundred dollars! Danni begged Mom to let her enter another pageant, then another, and soon Danni was the reigning beauty queen in her age range. Even better, Danni was bringing in enough money to allow Mom to quit her job at the daycare center and focus on helping Danni continue in the pageant world.

I never gave a hoot for any of that beauty stuff. One time Danni dragged me along to a class at a beauty salon where I managed to irritate the instructor so much that he whipped a handful of curlers at me and kicked me out of the class and the salon — forever.

Here's the part of my life where I have to talk about Robert.

Robert K. Ruebens is a music agent. He has made a lot of money helping other people make their musical dreams come true. Robert is okay-looking, but he spends so much time and money on his hair, teeth, and fancy clothes that he seems more handsome than he really is. I think Robert is a rat. Mom says that Robert is not a bad guy; it's just that he's so focused on his job that if you aren't directly related to what he's doing (making money), then he doesn't see you, hear you, or acknowledge your existence. In other words, he's rotten to me.

Mom likes to tell people it was fate that brought Robert into our lives; truth is, it was a junky car with a lame transmission and bad brakes.

Me, Mom, and Danni were in Los Angeles, California, so Danni could compete in the Miss Fifteen-and-Fabulous beauty pageant. Mom was driving up a steep hill when the transmission slipped and our car began to roll backward. Mom tried to stop, but the car kept going. It was scary; we all screamed, but the car didn't go very far. It only rolled a couple of feet — what stopped it was the car behind us. We rushed out of the car and found Robert sitting behind the wheel of his now-smooshed 1962 Mercedes Gull-wing convertible (it was a really cool car...*was*). Robert was shocked. Mom apologized over and over again. She was babbling about how sorry she was when reporters and television cameras began to descend on the scene. Suddenly a reporter shoved a microphone in Mom's face and asked her how it felt to have almost flattened one of the most powerful men in the music industry. Robert was pale and just kept repeating, "My baby, just out of the shop," in a trembling voice.

Not to brag, but it was me who saved the day. I walked over to Robert and told him that he should be grateful that he wasn't hurt. When he began to wail about how much it was going to cost to fix his car, I calmly explained that we had no money yet; however, Danni was going to be a superstar singer someday and if Robert were to represent her he'd get his car money, and a lot more.

Robert was so stunned by a little kid talking business that he stopped whining. He looked at Danni. She was pretty enough to be a pop star, but how did he know that she could sing? I convinced him to attend the pageant that night so he could see Danni up onstage and hear her sing in a real, live performance. Robert did, and the minute he heard Danni sing, he knew he'd found his next big star. Mom signed a big fat contract that very night.

For the past three months now, Danni has been working with the best producers to record the perfect CD. She just turned sixteen and Robert is about to release her music and send her on the road for a tour of every big mall in America! He keeps saying that Danni will be an instant smash! Radio stations around the world will play her music. Her videos will be shown day and night. Her CD will fly off music-store shelves. Her songs will be downloaded at the speed of light! If everything works out the way Robert has planned, by the time she turns seventeen, Danni Devine will be a worldwide sensation and the number-one superstar pop princess on the planet!

I don't know about all this. It sounds way too good to be true and I don't like the idea of Danni being gone for so long. If it all does happen, will it make our lives perfect? I mean, everyone dreams of being rich and famous, right? But what I wonder is, will it really work out that way in real life? Guess I'll just have to wait and see.

Sam sat very still. *Wow,* she thought, *he really did make it all happen. Robert may be a creep, but the man can do his job.*

She mulled over the blog entry. It did have an awful lot of personal stuff, but that's what journals were supposed to contain. Her thoughts were swirling around in her head. She could always leave it for now and discuss it with Olga in the morning. Yeah, that might be the best thing to do. As she continued thinking through the situation, Sam absent-mindedly reached out and grabbed her bottle of soda. She took her biggest, sloppiest slurp yet, and let out an immense burp, the kind that makes the walls shake and the windows rattle.

"Samantha!"

Sam slammed her hands over her mouth and tried not to giggle; she'd been busted!

CHAPTER 2

Slowly Sam turned in her chair to see her mom in the doorway. Rose had her hands on her hips and a very disgusted look on her face. It was hard for Sam to take her annoyance all that seriously when Rose was teetering dangerously on such high, spiky heels. Even so, Sam could see that she wasn't going to be able to joke her way out of this one.

"Sorry, Mom."

Rose wobbled into Sam's room, trying to appear parental while also trying not to trip over any of the boxes on the floor. "Young lady, what have I told you about drinking that junk before you go out in

public? Now you'll be all gassy."

Sam didn't do a very good job of looking apologetic. "I said sorry, but come on, it was one little burp."

"Honey," Rose said gently, "now that your sister is a big star, we all have to be careful. People will be watching us all the time, no matter where we are or what we're doing. From now on, we have to be our best selves every second of every minute of every day."

Sam turned back to her computer. "Okay, Mom, but remember, Danni is the beauty queen. I'm the beauty-school dropout."

Rose cracked a little smile. "Sam, all I ask is that you try. Don't forget, we don't know what we can do until we try."

Sam gave a big, slow nod with each phrase. "I know. I hear you. I'll try."

Rose leaned over and gave Sam an appreciative hug. "Sweetie, I understand it's not easy. We all have to learn to adjust, but it's worth it. For the little bit of privacy we give up, we get the freedom of not having to worry about needing rent money. And let's not forget how nice it will be for you to be able to go horseback riding without having to shovel horse poop for three hours beforehand. Hmm?" Rose smiled and playfully tapped Sam's nose, "You can't tell me that's a smell you're going to miss."

Sam looked up at her mom. "I've never complained about it. Besides, I really like having a job. I don't see why I should have to quit just because we aren't poor anymore."

There was a momentary pause as Rose struggled to find a way to respond.

"Sweetie," she said softly, "I applaud your work ethic, but it doesn't make sense for you to spend hours shoveling manure to earn the opportunity to ride horses, when we can easily pay for it now. You have to grasp how awful it would look for the little sister of a famous celebrity to be seen carting around wheelbarrows of pony poop. People would think you were being neglected. Imagine the headlines of those gossip magazines: '*Singer's Sister Stuck in Muck*'. Everyone will think I'm a terrible mother."

Rose noticed Sam staring at the ground with a glum expression; it was time to lighten the mood. Rose pinched her nostrils closed so that her voice resembled that of a little kid who had sucked in the helium from a balloon. "Maybe you don't recognize how horrific you smell when you come home, but believe me, Little Bit, anyone within a ten-mile radius sure does!" She let go of her nose and leaned over to give Sam a good-natured poke in the arm. "There are days when I think you secretly take pleasure in making me gag."

Sam opened her mouth to protest, but there was enough truth in that statement to keep her quiet. She batted her eyelashes and gave her mom an overly sincere grin.

Rose let out a big guffaw. "Don't waste that Little-Miss-Innocent face; you never know when you're really going to need it." She looked at her enormous turquoise bracelet that had a tiny timepiece hidden among all the big blue stones. Once her eyes focused and she realized how far behind schedule she was, her demeanor completely changed. She stood straight up, ran her fingers through her hair, and let out a determined sigh. Without looking at Sam, Rose headed toward the door.

"Time to fly, Little Bit. Get your hat and jacket. Robert is waiting to take us to the concert."

The mention of that name completely tweaked Sam. She grimaced. Her arms flew out in exasperation. "Why, Mom? Why can't we have one evening without him and his big ol' white teeth?"

The outburst so shocked Rose that she almost fell off her heels. Slowly she turned back to face Sam. "Excuse me? Have you forgotten everything that Robert has done for this family?"

"But, Mom, he hates me!"

Rose's face registered such shock that Sam was sorry the words had slipped out. She'd been doing a pretty good job of not whining about her dislike for Robert, but with all the chaos of Danni coming home, her emotions had gotten control of her tongue. It wasn't fair of Sam to be such a drama queen, at least, not tonight. She tried to tone it down. "Okay, okay, maybe not 'hates', but you know he doesn't like me."

Rose stared at her daughter. Sam was not the kind of kid to stir up trouble for no reason, and Robert wasn't exactly warm and fuzzy with her. Unfortunately, this was not the time to deal with the situation. Rose gazed at Sam with genuine care and a bit of guilt. She wanted to make Sam feel better, but if they didn't get moving,

they'd hurt Danni by arriving late at her concert, and as Rose had been having enough problems getting along with her eldest daughter lately, she certainly didn't need to create anymore tension between the two of them.

"Sugar, I know Robert sometimes runs roughshod over you. This very morning I told him that it was awful not to have pulled a fourth concert ticket for your friend Olga. But, Sweetie, you have to remember that he's not family. He is Danni's agent. He is the reason she has a career and we have a beautiful new home to move into tomorrow. Yes, he can be a bit rude and overbearing, but he's a great agent. Please, Samantha Sue, please try to get along with him, for Danni's sake, for my sake."

Sam wished she'd never brought it up. *Stupid Robert*, she thought, *even when he's not in the room he's messing up my life*. Sam nodded and gave Rose a weak, but genuine, smile.

Rose picked up Sam's new hat and jacket (the ones that matched Rose's outfit) off a box near the door. "Your ten-point-two minutes are up. We have to go."

Sam turned her chair and attention back to her computer. "Two minutes."

"Now, please, Samantha."

Sam begged while typing, "One minute, Mom. I need just one more minute."

"Samantha, now!"

Sam kept typing. "Tell you what, I'm willing to work with you on this. How's about…I'll come now, if you don't make me do the interview after the concert." Sam looked up at Rose. "I really don't want to be on TV or talk into a microphone or, you know, be on TV."

Rose was stunned. "Samantha Sue, what has gotten into you? Lately, everything's either a negotiation or a plea bargain. You may complain about Robert, but let me tell you, Little Bit, you're acting more like him every day. Between the two of you, I don't know if I'm the Momma Bear or Judge Judy!"

Sam reached over and held up a book from a pile on her desk. "This," she declared, "is *The Art of the Deal*. It's all about negotiating and making deals and finding a win-win outcome for every situation."

Rose crossed her arms in front of her. "A win-win outcome?"

Sam nodded her most grown-up nod. "Yes. As the book's author, the world famous multi-gabillionaire,

Mister Donald Trump, says, a win-win outcome is when both parties involved in the dispute or negotiation find a solution that makes everyone happy; you know, where everybody gets something they want, so nobody feels like a total loser."

Rose eyed the book suspiciously. "And just where did we get this fine tome? I thought you only read biographies or horse stories."

Sam hung her head and sheepishly admitted, "Robert left it on the kitchen table last week. I figured I'd hold on to it for him, so it wouldn't get lost with all the packing."

Rose gave her daughter an "I-am-not-buying-this" look.

Sam knew she was on thin ice. "Mom," she said innocently, "you want me to make an effort to get along with the guy, so I figured by reading one of his books it…um…it might help me build a bridge. You know, have something to discuss with him."

Rose lowered her head so that she was peering at Sam through a disapproving scowl. Her voice was low, steady, and way too calm. "Samantha Sue Devine, I love you more than hot chocolate on a cold day, but you are pushing your luck. You snagged that book just to annoy Robert, but I don't care right now. The only thing I do care about at this moment is that your sister has a big show tonight, and we are not going to be late. I am now officially ten seconds away from losing my cool."

Rose tossed the hat and jacket to Sam, turned in a huff, and was just about to step outside Sam's room when she grabbed the door frame and swung herself back around.

"Little Bit, I'm going to tell you the very thing I told Robert this morning: not everything in life is negotiable. Sometimes you have to suck it up and accept a situation for what it is, and the situation here is that we have to go now, and you are doing the interview later."

Sam looked up at Rose with puppy-dog eyes and made a pathetic whimpering sound.

Rose hit her limit. "Enough, Samantha! You know that Danni is excited about doing the live interview, and you know that those TV people demanded that the entire family be in on it. You also know that I spent a great deal of time finding matching outfits for the three

of us, and believe me, Little Bit, trying to find something that pleases everyone in this family is not as easy as it used to be!"

Sam jumped up pleadingly. "I know, Mom, but the jacket is itchy and the hat is too big!"

Rose closed her eyes, put the back of her hand to her forehead, and spoke to herself in a loud whisper. "I am calm and in control. I am calm and in control." She opened her eyes and looked at Sam with a forced smile. She spoke in an eerily cheerful voice. "My child, I am now going to walk to our front door and count to three. If you are not by my side, at our door, by the time I reach the number three, I can guarantee, beyond any shadow of a doubt, that it'll be coal for Christmas and buh-bye to your birthday."

She slammed the door. Sam raced back to her computer. She typed one last thought in her blog.

This is starting out as one massive lose-lose kind
of night.
:-(
Gotta go!
TTFN!

She hit the "send" button just as she heard Rose yell, "One!" from the hallway.

"Come on! Post, blog, post!" Sam pleaded as she pulled on the crumpled jacket and flattened the too-big hat on her too-little head.

"Two!"

Sam was sweating as the hourglass on her computer screen spun to show that her blog was being uploaded to the server.

"Two and a half!"

Sam slammed down the purple lid of her laptop just as the screen flashed, "Upload complete." She raced to the front door and was at Rose's side so fast that even Rose was surprised.

"Thr— Nice save, Little Bit."

CHAPTER 3

Sam felt like a complete goof riding in the back of the Hummer limo. *Leave it to Robert,* she thought, *to get the biggest, ugliest, barf-green limo in the whole world.* Sam had secretly dreamed of riding in a beautiful, white limousine with a sunroof so she could stand up and take digital photos with Olga's cell phone, but Robert had managed to ruin that by putting her into something so totally gross, that even if it had a sunroof (which it didn't), she'd have been too mortified to let people see her inside it. She looked out the window and gasped as the limo turned a corner and she saw the huge crowd outside the stadium.

"All these people are here to see Danni?" she blurted out, not meaning to actually voice what she was thinking.

Robert smugly replied without looking at her, "Kid, you have no idea how big your sister is."

Sam was about to snap at him that she wasn't a kid, but she noticed that Rose seemed kind of nervous, so Sam bit her lip and didn't say a word.

The limo pulled around the back of the stadium and a group of burly guards cleared a path so they could exit the Hummer monstrosity. They were right in the middle of the roped-off red carpet. Sam almost biffed it as she climbed (more like fell) out of the giant limo because all the flashbulbs flashing, the people yelling, and the insane energy of the whole scene completely took her breath away. It was seriously wild.

Robert was flashing his million-dollar grin for all to behold. Sam rolled her eyes as she watched him lift his wrist to his mouth to bark another order into his wrist-phone. He is such a creep, she thought, he really believes that he is too important to have to waste time taking a cell phone out of his pocket like a normal person. Sam didn't realize that she was actually glaring

at Robert until he turned to face her. She quickly looked down.

Robert shoved a small piece of plastic with a flimsy chain at her. She saw the words "Backstage Pass – All Access" on it. As usual, he spoke without looking at her.

"You know what this is," he snapped. "Do not lose it!"

Sam gave him a super-fake smile and put the pass around her neck. She was examining it when she heard someone calling her name. Sam scanned the crowd and caught sight of her best friend's chubby, round face grinning at her.

"Sam! Hey, Sam!" Olga yelled. "Over here! *Sam!*"

Sam grabbed Rose's arm. "Mom, it's Olga! Can I go talk to her?"

"Sure, Sweetie," Rose said, relieved that Sam was finally showing some enthusiasm, "but just for a minute. I don't want to lose you in this crowd."

Sam elbowed her way to the edge of the red carpet. "Olga, I am so glad to see you!" she gushed. "Even my mom ripped on Robert for not getting you a ticket. I so wish you could have come with us. I could totally use somebody on my side tonight."

38

Olga laughed. "I know the feeling. Listen, it was really tough getting here! Even with all my dad's TV-director buddies and my mom's modeling connections, we had to buy our tickets from an online auction, and they were expensive! And look who demanded to tag along." Olga rolled her eyes as she tipped her head to the left, directing Sam's eyes over to Inga, Olga's bratty ten-year-old sister.

Sam saw Inga, dressed in one of her usual trendy, expensive designer outfits, flick her hand at her in some kind of half-hearted little wave. The sight of a signal of acknowledgment from Inga was so unexpected that Sam squinted to be sure her eyes weren't playing tricks on her.

"Is she waving hello to me?" Sam asked incredulously.

Olga stared intently at Inga. "Well, it appears to be a wave-like gesture, but I've never seen her show friendship or kindness to anyone, so I can't be completely sure."

Sam was stunned. In the four years since she and Olga had first met at the stables and immediately become best friends, Inga had always acted better,

smarter, and way cooler than everyone, especially Sam. Seeing Inga looking right at her and making a social gesture was startling. Sam forced a grin, but through her teeth asked, "Is she kidding me?"

Olga sighed. "Anything is possible; she's acting totally out of character. Miss Thing pitched the biggest *hissy* you could imagine to get permission to come and see Danni tonight. Even I was impressed by her world-class display of spoiled-rottenness."

"Yikes! That's really saying something!"

Olga faced Sam head on. "I know! That's what I'm trying to tell you! Your sister has become a major star. She's a seriously big somebody!"

Sam nodded. "Yeah, but thankfully, as of tomorrow, Miss Big Somebody will go back to being normal Miss Big Sister Normal-Nobody."

Olga blinked twice; her eyes popped wide open with surprise. "You don't really believe that, do you? Look around, Sam. *Danni is a star!* She can't just disappear into her old life like none of this ever happened. Besides, you think Robert would give up on his mega-moneymaker that easily?"

Sam cringed. "Please, don't mention that name.

I am so not liking anything about him right now. He treats me like I'm some old piece of furniture he'd happily donate to Goodwill."

Olga giggled. "I hear you. The only thing my mom's modeling agent ever says to me is," Olga's voice took on a perfect New York accent, "'You – small person – coffee – two sugars – pronto!'"

Sam nodded understandingly, not finding the situation as entertaining as Olga. "It's, like, I know he's good at his job, but I don't see how anybody can trust a person whose teeth are that white. It's not normal. Every time he smiles I get a ripping headache."

A tiny titter escaped Olga's lips. "Yeah, but you have to admit he's kind of hot...for an old guy." Olga stepped closer to Sam. "Look at him," she whispered in Sam's ear. "He's tall, but not too tall, got great shoulders, and big, beautiful brown eyes. Yeah, those pearly whites *are* too much, but how can you not see that he is genuinely *fine*?"

"*Ewww*," Sam cringed. "Stop that! Listen, you want hot? After the concert, we're doing that interview for TV, and guess what channel it's for!"

Olga's eyes widened. "No!"

Sam beamed with pride. "Yup! Today's 2 Cool Teens Network! And so you know who is doing the interviewing, don't you?"

Olga's eyes got even bigger and wider. "No!"

Sam's smile grew even bigger as she nodded her best "Oh-you-better-believe-it-baby" nod.

Olga was beside herself with excitement and envy. "No way!"

Sam's face hurt from grinning so broadly. It felt good to be the person doing the cool thing for once.

Olga gave Sam a friendly slug on the arm. "See, I told you awesome stuff would come out of this. I can't believe you get to meet Marty Meister! I swear, he is the best thing about that whole 2 Cool Teens Network." Olga sniffled and put her hand to her heart. "And to think I was worried about how you were going to deal with Danni and all the weirdness her new life would bring." She gave Sam her most dramatic face. "And now you get to hang out with the hunkiest dude on TV, 'The Meisternator' himself! Life is so unfair." Olga tried to wipe away a fake tear, but she was laughing too hard at her own silliness to pull it off.

Sam giggled along, "Okay, Drama Girl, I'll call

you from Hawaii if Marty and I elope."

Suddenly, Sam stopped giggling and got very quiet. This was supposed to be a fun night, so why was she feeling so anxious and uncomfortable? "You might be right," she said softly, "I really hope you're right. Maybe all this showbiz stuff won't be so bad."

Seeing Sam getting way too serious, Olga gave her a second friendly slug on the arm. "Hey! Where's the cell phone? Did you take any pictures for your blog?"

That snapped Sam out of her somber moment. "I wanted to, but *Guess-Who* managed to find us the one limo in the whole world without a sunroof! I'll get some photos backstage with Danni after the concert. Think you could meet me back here? I'll take you with me to the interview and Danni's party!"

Before Olga could reply, a slightly older girl with bright red hair and even brighter red rubber bands on her gigantic braces butted into the conversation.

"Whoa! Did I hear you say something about a party and Danni?" she spat out at Sam.

Olga gave Sam a look to try to tell her to be careful, but Sam didn't notice.

"Yup." Sam nodded. "She's my sister!"

"Whoa! I didn't know Danni had a sister." Brace-face stared at Sam. "You don't look like her. You sure you're Danni Devine's sister?"

"Yeah," Sam laughed, "I'm sure. How else do you think I got this?"

Sam held up her backstage pass. Olga shot Sam a second warning look that Sam again failed to notice. Having a successful Mexican-TV-director dad and a celebrated-fashion-model mom, Olga had been living in the world of rich and famous people her whole life. She was never comfortable being the kid who had more money than everyone else, and had learned long ago that some people would pretend to be her friend in an effort to get closer to her parents. Unlike Inga who loved being treated as if she were a princess, Olga preferred to blend in and not call attention to herself. Olga had learned to trust her gut instincts about people and their true intentions; something about this exchange was making her uncomfortable.

Brace-face stepped a little closer to Sam. "Whoa! That's unreal!"

Olga's trouble radar was going off; she just knew this wasn't going to end well. She gave a loud cough to get Sam's attention and glared at her friend, trying to warn her to be careful. Sam, never being the kid anybody wanted anything from, had no idea why Olga was making such a bizarre face. Besides, she was enjoying the attention.

Sam smiled and held out the pass for Brace-face to see. "It's pretty cool, isn't it?"

Brace-face reached out to touch the pass. Suddenly, she tightened her grip, ripped it off Sam's neck, and vanished into the crowd.

"Ouch!" Sam yelled out before realizing what had happened. "Come back! Give that back! Oh, man, *come back*!"

Sam bit her bottom lip and closed her eyes tightly. When she opened them, she hoped and prayed the pass would still be around her neck, but that was one wish that was never going to come true. *Dead*, she thought, *I'm dead, D-E-A-D exclamation mark. I am dead.* She sheepishly looked at Olga who was being sympathetic, but realistic.

"Oh, Sam," she said sadly, "you are so going to get it."

Sam attempted to think positive. "Um, maybe with

everything that's going on, nobody will notice?"

Olga knew that was never going to happen. "Yeah, sure. You hold on to that thought."

Sam felt a thump on the head. She glanced up to see Robert actually focusing on her.

"Move it, Squirt," he snarled. "We needed to be in our seats five minutes ago. Your…"

It figured that the one time Robert paid any attention to Sam would be when she'd messed up. He noticed the missing backstage pass and the red mark around her neck. "Again?" he growled. "Already?" Robert shook his head in utter disgust.

Sam turned to Olga, who waved goodbye. "It's okay, Sam," she called out as she began to move back into the crowd, dragging Inga away from the paparazzi. "I'll catch you later. Call me if you don't get home too late. I want to know where to send you and Marty your wedding presents."

Sam waved back and was about to respond when Robert spun her around by the shoulder and pushed her down the red carpet. Rose was smiling as she waited for them at the security entrance, until she noticed that Sam was looking down and rubbing a red mark on her neck. Rose opened her mouth to speak, but Robert had to get in the first word.

"Well, I suppose we are making progress. That backstage pass lasted almost five minutes." He shot Rose a glare that made his annoyance very clear.

Rose gave Sam a little hug and one of those gentle "it's okay" expressions that moms are so good at. Sam was about to explain what had happened when she heard a massive cheer from inside the stadium. Robert hustled her and Rose to their seats in the darkness. Just as Sam sat down, a giant pink spotlight appeared in the center of the empty stage.

Immediately, Sam was overcome with excitement. She'd seen Danni perform a million times, but never in a place this immense, and for so many people. Fog rolled out over the stage. Danni appeared as if by magic in the middle of the pink spotlight, and the crowd went nuts! The cheering was deafening. The scene took Sam's breath away and, for the first time, she saw her sister as "Danni Devine, Superstar." It was exciting and overwhelming.

The next two hours were a complete blur. Every note Danni sang, every move she made, the crowd cheered, whistled, and applauded. People were singing along, dancing in their seats, and screaming uncontrollably.

And then, after three encores, the show was over. Robert hustled them out of their seats. As they made their way through the crowd, Sam held on to the back of Rose's jacket and looked down so she wouldn't get elbowed in the head. This let her focus on what she was hearing. People were going on and on about what an amazing concert it had been and how talented and beautiful Danni was. Sam must have heard at least a dozen young girls squealing about how they had to get Danni's autograph. *This is all too freaky*, Sam thought to herself; *it's a good thing it'll all be over tomorrow*!

CHAPTER 4

By the time Robert got Rose and Sam through the crowd, backstage, and out the secret door that led to the huge tent behind the stadium, Danni was already in the middle of her live TV interview. She and Marty "The Meisternator" Meister, the hottest guy on TV, were sitting on tall director's chairs over in a corner of the tent. They were completely surrounded by the TV crew. Robert pushed everyone aside so he and Rose and Sam were up front, just out of camera range. Sam gasped when she saw her sister. Danni was seriously stunning. Her hair seemed longer and shinier than Sam remembered and the makeup made her blue eyes look even bluer. Danni was wearing a jacket and hat similar to Sam's, but everything actually fit Danni and looked good on her. Sam pulled the too-big hat off her head and tried to smooth her rumpled jacket. As she was fidgeting, Robert thumped her on the head again.

"Hey!" he hissed. "Be still."

Sam gave him a snotty look, but she stood still. Marty was asking Danni questions while pointing at old video clips playing on a huge screen between them. Sam almost laughed out loud when she recognized the first video; it was an old tape of Danni winning the Little Miss Three Rivers beauty pageant.

"How many of these kiddy beauty pageants did you win?" Marty asked Danni.

Danni reached her hand back and tossed her long, silky hair over her shoulder in a move that looked rehearsed to Sam.

"Oh, my, I don't know. I guess maybe like fifteen, sixteen. At some point we stopped counting." She flashed a perfect grin at Marty.

"Actually," Marty said, more to the TV camera than to Danni, "you won exactly twenty-four pageants between the ages of ten and fifteen."

"Well, if you say so, I guess it must be true!" Danni beamed back.

Sam wondered why her sister was acting so bizarrely, and then it hit her. Danni was flirting with Marty! *Wow,* she thought, *that's guts!* Marty was so totally gorgeous that Sam could barely imagine talking to the guy, let alone flirting with him on live TV.

"And you made the leap from beauty pageants to pop singing when you were…?" Marty waited for a reply when it was perfectly obvious that he already knew the answer.

Danni pretended to have to work hard to think about this. *That is so fake*, Sam said to herself, *as if she doesn't remember the exact moment! It was only like the most important event of her entire life so far.*

Danni turned in her chair and waved at Robert. "Hey, Robert!" she yelled out. "Do you remember when I made the leap from pageant girl to pop singer?"

"Indeed I do," answered Robert loudly enough for the microphones to pick up. He stepped onto the set and stood next to Danni's chair. "That was a rather memorable day." Robert flashed that expensive pearly smile he was so fond of, and Sam wondered if the glare

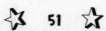

would blind any of the viewers at home.

The giant screen behind Danni and Marty now began playing the tape made by those TV reporters that fateful day when the Devine family had met Robert Ruebens. It showed a reporter standing in front of Robert's smooshed 1962 Mercedes Gull-wing convertible with Rose's heap of a car rolled on top of the front end.

"We are here at the scene of a dangerously close call for top music star-maker Robert Ruebens." The reporter was pathetically serious about such a no-big-deal news story. She stuck the microphone in Robert's face. "Mr. Ruebens, how does it feel to have cheated death?"

Robert wasn't even aware that a microphone was in his face. He didn't look up, but kept his sad eyes on his car and just kept repeating, "My baby, just out of the shop."

Behind Robert stood Rose, a fifteen-year-old Danni, and a ten-year-old Sam, huddled together, waiting to see what would happen next.

Sam abruptly stepped forward and yelled out, "Momma said she was sorry, Mister!"

The video stopped; everyone on the set laughed, except for Sam. She didn't understand what was so funny. She was relieved when the laughter died down and Marty finally spoke again.

"And so, after that rather inauspicious meeting, Mr. Ruebens became your agent?" he asked.

"That's right," Robert chimed in. "I know star quality, and I recognized it the minute I laid eyes on Miss Devine here."

Yeah, right, Sam thought to herself, *after I got you to quit whining about your stupid car and dragged your sorry self over to the beauty pageant!*

Over the next couple of minutes Danni, Marty, and Robert discussed how quickly things had changed for Danni once her CD had been released. There were more video clips that illustrated how almost overnight, Danni had gone from singing in front of eight people at a tiny shopping mall in Des Moines to performing for thousands of screaming fans inside the gigantic Mall of America.

Marty noticed the director waving at him, so he abruptly turned his focus away from Danni and spoke directly to the TV camera.

"So, after an amazing year that took her from hometown beauty queen to international singing sensation, what's next for this superstar? Stay tuned! We'll be right back to talk to Danni and her family."

From behind the camera, the director yelled, "And we're out. Sixty seconds, people! Get the family in place!"

Three more tall director's chairs were put on the set. Rose was escorted over to her chair next to Danni. Robert oozed his way over to his chair on the other side. Two guys rushed over to powder and preen both Danni and Rose. Sam noticed that Rose and Danni smiled at each other, but neither said a word; there was definite tension between the two of them. *What is going on with them?* she wondered. *Mom and Danni never used to fight, but ever since Danni left on tour, they can't seem to get along. Every phone call seems to end with one of them hanging up on the other. Maybe it was just the distance. Maybe now that Danni will be home, things will calm back down.* Still thinking about the strange behavior of her mom and sister, Sam took a few steps to head to her chair, but she got lost in the shuffle of people, so she hopped over to the side to wait for the crowd to thin out. She took a long look at her sister whom she hadn't seen in person for a couple of months. It was Danni, to be sure, but she looked kind of different and she was sure acting, well, not like the normal Danni. Sam noticed that Danni kept looking at Marty out of the corner of her eye, even when Robert spoke to her.

"That was brilliant, Danni. Excellent job! You're working the camera beautifully."

Danni responded to Robert, but kept her gaze fixed on Marty. "Thank you, Robert. You know, it's easy when you have such an amazing professional interviewer asking the questions."

Marty didn't hear a word Danni said. He was too focused on staring at his perfect self in a mirror. Sam was about to laugh at this when she suddenly felt her arm being practically yanked out of its socket.

"Hey!" she yelled. "Let me go!"

A security guard was holding Sam's arm rather firmly and looking as if he were about to toss her out a back door.

"This is a restricted area, little girl!" he bellowed down at her. "And I don't see no pass, so you gotta go!"

Danni jumped up from her chair and waved. "No! No! It's cool! That's my little sister! She's with me! Let her go."

Sam wrestled her arm free of the guard's grip. She straightened her jacket as smugly as possible and haughtily announced, "That's correct. I'm with her!"

She picked up her hat and strutted onto the set. Sam had been thinking of all kinds of clever things to say to Danni when she finally got to see her again, but once she was next to her, she was so overcome that she couldn't say anything. She threw her arms around her big sister and gave her one of the all-time greatest hugs.

Danni was surprisingly emotional about seeing Sam again. She did a good job of keeping her cool, but her voice was more than a little quivery as she hugged back and said, "Yeah, I missed you too, Little Bit."

"Watch the jacket, Squirt!" growled Robert. "Your sister doesn't need to be on live TV covered in kid snot."

Sam stared into Danni's eyes. "How come your eyes look so…"

Danni batted her lashes, "Beautiful?"

Sam stared harder. "No, bluer."

Danni giggled. "I'm wearing colored contacts."

Sam didn't understand. "But you've never needed glasses."

At this, the two young men touching up Danni's hair and makeup chortled out loud. Sam tilted her head to look up at them and was surprised to see that they seemed to be exactly alike; the only thing different was that one guy was dressed all in black and the other was in brown from head to toe.

The guy in brown spoke without looking at Sam. "Zees contacts are not for seeing good, zey are for looking good."

Sam scrunched up her face as she tried to figure out what Mr. Brown Outfit had said to her. Danni tittered at Sam's bewilderment. "Sam, meet the most important people on my support team. This is Jean and Jehan Tissaire; the *très* hottest hair and makeup artists in show business. Robert brought them over all the way from Paris, France! Aren't they fabulous?"

Sam looked back and forth, from Jean to Jehan, or Jehan to Jean; she seriously could not tell them apart. "I'm guessing you guys are twins?"

Both men stopped dead in their tracks, put their hands on their hips, and looked at each other as if they had just heard the dopiest thing ever.

The one dressed all in black finally spoke. "Why do people always assume zat?"

The one dressed in brown responded, "I will never understand. Look at us, we are more different zen day and night!"

Sam laughed out loud at the obvious humor in that oh-so-wrong statement, until she realized that the brothers were serious! She cringed in embarrassment as they stared at her. She had to change the subject super-fast.

"Um," she stammered, "Danni, your hair looks really awesome. I don't remember it ever being so long."

The brother dressed all in black beamed with pride. "Zat is my doing!" He ran his fingers through Danni's blonde locks. "I spent weeks searching for ze most perfect hair extensions to make our Mz. Danni look so gorgeous!"

Sam looked at her sister. "Fake contacts, fake hair? It is really you inside there, isn't it?"

Danni was taken aback by the comment. Sam could see her sister was trying to figure out if she should feel insulted. Jean and Jehan both froze and waited for Danni's reaction.

Danni looked squarely at Sam and began to howl with laughter. Jean and Jehan joined in with a giggle; they shared a quick look of relief and got back to the business of primping Danni.

"That was funny, Little Bit," Danni managed to get out in-between peals of laughter. "I'd forgotten how funny you can be!"

Before Sam could respond, the director yelled out, "Twenty seconds, people! Everyone but the family and Marty, please clear the set."

Before turning to get into her chair, Sam sneaked a peek at Marty. Danni caught her and whispered, "He is a hottie, isn't he?"

Sam, noticing Marty was still focused on his reflection in the mirror, replied, "He sure seems to think so."

Both sisters giggled, but were quickly hushed up by the director yelling, "Ten seconds!"

Danni sat back in her chair, but couldn't resist

getting in a good-natured sisterly dig. She smirked as she prepared to needle Sam with something she knew would make her go nuts.

"So, Sam, between my show and your being on TV, you should finally have something interesting to write in your little *blag*."

Sam was having trouble trying to climb up onto her chair (why did they make those things so tall, anyway?) but she couldn't not respond to Danni's teasing. "Aurgh! It's called a blog, Miss Tech-Know-Nothing. A *blog*!"

Suddenly, Sam's chair collapsed into a heap on the floor. Everybody froze. Sam was about to bend over and try to fix the stupid thing when the director yelled out: "FIVE...four...three..."

Robert rose from his chair, tossed Sam into his seat, plopped the hat on her head, kicked her chair out of the way, and stood where her chair had been – smiling that big white smile.

The director pointed at Marty and the interview continued as if nothing unusual had happened.

"Welcome back to T2CT's 'How They Got To Be Hot'. I'm Marty 'The Meisternator' Meister, and

we're at the wrap party for Danni Devine's 'Malls Across America' tour with the superstar and her family. Danni, please introduce everyone."

Danni made a grand gesture of tossing out a perfectly manicured hand toward Rose. "Well, Marty, this is my beautiful mother and wonderful manager, Rose."

Rose smiled and waved at the camera as gracefully as the Queen of England.

Danni then made another grand gesture toward Robert. "And you already know my absolutely brilliant agent, the one, the only, Mr. Robert Ruebens."

Robert flashed his best, "How are ya, babe" smile at the camera.

Danni clasped her hands in front of her and lowered her chin in a very mischievous way. "And last, but, of course, not least, is my little bit of a little sister, Sam."

Sam gave a pathetic grin and a single, unenthusiastic wave. *That was not the most exciting introduction*, she thought to herself. *Mom gets "beautiful," Robert gets "brilliant," and all I get is "little bit of a little sister."* At least with the stupid hat covering her eyes, Sam couldn't see everyone staring at her, and that was more than fine with her.

Of course, the second Sam thought about the hat, Rose noticed it hanging over her face. She swiftly reached over and yanked it back as Marty began speaking.

"So, Rose, how do you deal with being both a mom and a manager?"

Rose pulled her hand away from Sam's hat and sat up straight. She spoke to the camera in a voice that was unnaturally sweet.

"I make an effort to find balance, Marty," Rose cooed. "That's what it's all about, balance and boundaries. I try to ensure that Danni has time to relax and be a teenager while still doing everything it takes to be a superstar. Sometimes, it's not easy. Just this morning Robert and I had quite a serious conversation, trying to hammer out the details for an exciting new opportunity for Danni. When it seems like everyone in the world wants to know everything there is to know about a person, you have to figure out where to draw the line. Isn't that right, Robert?"

Robert kept smiling, but it was obvious from the look in his eye that Rose had said something that hadn't exactly pleased him.

Robert laughed. "Everything worth doing requires a little give and take. There's nothing a good agent enjoys more than an intense negotiation."

Sam could tell there was more going on here than just what Robert and Rose were saying. Rose was still smiling, but the look in her eyes wasn't quite right. Maybe this was why Rose had gotten so snarky before they'd left for the concert. Maybe Sam's trying to weasel more time out of Rose had reminded her of some negotiation or fight she was having with Robert over some new deal for Danni. Sam made a mental note to try and figure out later what Robert and Rose were fighting about.

Marty nodded as if he was listening (which he wasn't) and turned his attention to Sam. He froze for a moment; Sam realized that he had forgotten her name.

"So...little sister," Marty stammered, "you must get a lot of tips on performing from your big sis. Will you be following in her singing and dancing footsteps soon?"

Sam was so surprised by the question that she snorted. "No way! I'm going to be a world-famous writer and an Olympic barrel buster!"

Marty was confused. "A barrel buster? Like, with horses?"

Sam stared at him incredulously. "Like, yes? Horses go around the barrel, like, barrel-busting. Duh." She shook her head in disbelief. How could he not know this?

Marty looked around the set for someone to help him. He hadn't expected the kid to go off on another topic. "Uh...okay...I didn't know barrel-riding was an Olympic sport."

Danni chimed in. "It's not," she said, looking directly at Sam.

Sam knew she was getting shot down. She glared at Danni as if to say, "Thanks a lot."

Danni glared back, but said, "I mean, it's not an Olympic sport...yet."

Sam saw that Danni was just giving her a hard time and smiled a great big "Thanks." For a moment, Sam forgot about the TV cameras and all the strangers. It was just her and Danni, being sisters and hanging out. Then Robert *had* to speak.

"Yes, yes, we all have exciting plans for the future. In fact," he babbled on, "we are all particularly excited about tomorrow."

Marty looked relieved not to have to talk to Sam anymore. "Yeah, we hear that you're moving into a new home—"

"A house!" Sam yelled out before she could stop herself. "A huge house! Mom says it's got a swimming pool, and a big backyard, and—"

"AND we're out of time!" Marty was relieved to get the "end it" signal from the director. He'd had enough of this goofy kid and just wanted out of there. "Thank you, Danni Devine for letting us know the real you a little better."

Danni beamed her beauty-queen smile. "It's been my pleasure, Marty. I'm always happy to chat with any of my T2CT friends."

Marty gave a nod as he thanked Robert and Rose but, again, when he got to Sam, he forgot her name and froze.

Sam sighed and then very slowly, making sure to exaggerate every sound, she practically shouted, "S-A-M."

Only those people who were really paying attention caught the harsh look Marty threw Sam's way before turning to the camera. "And for Today's 2 Cool Teens

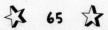

Network, this is Marty 'The Meisternator' Meister. Good-times and goodnight!"

Everyone sat, smiling, waiting for the red light on top of the camera to go off and the director to yell "Cut," when, suddenly, with no warning, Sam felt a little rumble in her stomach. Before she could catch herself, Sam let out a gigantic burp. Horrified, her hands flew up to her mouth and her eyes squeezed shut. She heard Marty laughing. She heard Rose let out a deep, disappointed sigh. She heard Danni gasp, but the thing that really killed her was just after the director finally yelled, "We're out," hearing Robert say, "Of course she did!" loud enough for everybody on the set to hear.

CHAPTER 5

Click click click, clack clack click.

I wanted to post this last night, but by the time I got home from the great "interview nightmare", I was too fried to even think straight. I can't believe I burped on live TV. The rest of the night, everybody cracked up whenever I walked by. I was so bummed by it all that I didn't even take a single digital picture. Mom didn't say a thing about the burp, but the minute we got home she walked into my room and took away my bottle of orange cream soda (sigh). Got a text message on

the cell phone from Olga saying that she saw the interview and the burp wasn't THAT loud (Thanks, Olga!).

Mom and Danni had a weird moment after the interview. Mom said something about Danni needing to leave the after-concert party and go to sleep. Danni snottily replied that since it was her party, she could stay as late as she wanted. For a moment, I thought they were going to start yelling at each other, but Robert jumped in and negotiated some truce where Danni got to stay at the party for another hour. I hope that now Danni is home for good, all her bizarre tension with Mom will end. I don't like the two of them not getting along. It makes my stomach hurt.

Whatever... I've got more important stuff to think about. I mean, this is it! MOVING DAY!! I'm all ready, except for my computer (duh).
;-)

One more thing, I heard Mom and Robert talking

super-serious this morning. I walked into the kitchen and they both totally clammed up. I hate when adults do that. Like I'm not smart enough to figure out that they only stopped talking because I walked into the room. I can't imagine what could be such a big deal. We've got the new house, we're moving today, and Danni's finally home. So, what's the stinky secret???? Whatever it is, I guess I don't care that much... at least not right now. All I care about is that we are moving in to a new house and a totally new and exciting part of our lives. How cool is that? Now Danni is home and Mom won't have to work so hard, and we get a house with a swimming pool, and I finally, finally, FINALLY get my own bedroom (I'm hoping for bright purple walls and light purple carpet) and, best of all, we get to be a normal family again. Big yea! Photos to follow soon – I promise!

Sam hit "send" just as Robert shouted for everyone to meet him outside at the limo that very minute. Sam peeked out her window – *the last time I'll peek out this window*, she thought – and saw Robert looking at his watch, tapping the roof of the limo in agitation, and looking at his watch again. *At least the creep finally got a normal limo with a sunroof,* Sam conceded. Robert yelled out once more for the family to get outside. Sam mocked him as he did, making an exaggerated face and flapping her lips and, of course, he glanced up and caught her. His sour expression showed a clear lack of amusement. Sam slunk back in and packed up her computer, all the while praying Robert wouldn't tell Rose what she'd done. This was to be a great morning, a fresh start with the new house and all, and Sam didn't want to move in to her new home with her mom already disappointed in her.

Sam rushed out of the apartment and down the stairs. Robert was bounding up the stairs and practically tripped over her. They both stood in the stairwell, waiting for the other to apologize. Neither one did. It was Danni, shrieking a horrified, "Eek!" from outside, who broke the tension of the moment.

Robert and Sam both rushed out to the driveway where Danni was standing next to the limo with a

look of utter terror on her face. Danni was holding out a cardboard cup as if it were a giant spider about to bite her.

Robert looked genuinely concerned. "What? What's happened? Talk to me, Danni! Whatever it is, Robert can fix it!"

Danni let out a heartfelt sob. "Oh, Robert, I went for a little walk to clear my head and say goodbye to the old neighborhood."

"Yes, yes, go on." Robert was completely focused on Danni.

"And," Danni continued after another sob, "and I popped into a café to get my morning pick-me-up, you know, like I did every morning on the road."

"Yes, I know," Robert cooed. "Go on. What happened?"

"Well, I got my drink and a few kids followed me out the door and all the way here."

"Yes, go on," Robert purred.

"And so I didn't get to taste my drink until just now and, and, and—"

"And…" Robert asked with a tremor of fear in his voice.

"And," wailed Danni, "and I just know this mocha chai latte has *real milk* in it!"

Give me a break, Sam thought to herself as she rolled her eyes.

"That is unforgivable," declared Robert as he removed the offending cup from Danni's trembling hand. "Let Robert take care of this!"

Robert raised his wrist to his mouth and began barking into that ever-present wrist-phone, "Judy! Judy! I need a large SOY mocha chai latte here at the Devines' old place. Now!" He turned his attention to Danni. "Relax, Danni. You need to get yourself centered."

Sam couldn't believe how silly this was. "Oh, please," she said to her still-sobbing sister. "When did you become such a big baby?"

Danni turned red. "Zip it, Little Bit! I wrote you about my lactose intolerance two months ago when I discovered it!"

Sam laughed. "Yeah, right. Wasn't that just after you saw that interview where Lady Gaga went on and on about giving up cheese because she didn't like its karma? Get a grip. You've been eating ice cream your

whole life and one morning you wake up and decide you're suddenly this delicate flower?"

"I'll have you know that I was diagnosed by the top aura reader!" Danni spat at her little sister.

Sam looked at Danni as if she was crazy. "What?"

Danni flipped her hair over her shoulder. "When I was doing that talk show in Chicago, one of the other guests was the aura reader to the stars, and she told me that dairy is only good for people who have blue in their auras. Mine is bright yellow. That means I am extremely incapable of properly digesting any milk products."

Sam shook her head. "I so don't buy this."

Robert, of course, had to get involved. "Excuse me, Doctor," he said sarcastically, "I'll have you know that lactose intolerance is a serious medical condition and I will thank you not to upset your sister right now."

"This is so uncool!" Sam turned to march back into the apartment. She had to ask Rose when Danni had become such a spoiled brat. But before she could take two steps, she had to jump out of the way to avoid getting run over by a delivery guy racing up the driveway with one hand on his handlebars and the other holding out a huge paper cup.

Robert threw open his arms. "*Voilà!*" He tipped the delivery guy and handed Danni the cup. "Here you go, my dear. All is well. Now you settle into the limo and pull yourself together."

Sam made loud barfing noises, but Robert and Danni ignored her.

"Furthermore," Robert continued, "we have quite a day ahead of us and you need to look your best for your fans."

Sam didn't like the sound of that. "What are you talking about? We're just going to the new house, right? This is a family day, right?" She stepped suspiciously toward Robert.

Robert saw trouble, so he quickly yelled, "Rose! We need to leave! We're off schedule!"

But Sam wasn't prepared to back down. "What do you mean 'off schedule'? We're just going to the new house, right? What kind of schedule do we have? This is our day, Robert. It has nothing to do with you. This is our day, right?"

Rose suddenly appeared, looking like a person who had taken a great deal of time and care with her appearance. It was pretty obvious she wasn't wearing your typical "moving day" kind of outfit.

"Good morning, everyone!" she sang out. "Sorry to be a tad late, but I'm here now and ready to go."

Even Danni was stunned into silence by Rose's dress and demeanor. Rose swept past everyone and glided into the limo as gracefully as a prima ballerina.

Danni and Sam exchanged looks; they both knew something was up.

Robert ushered them to the open limo door. "Let's go, please. Now. No talking, no questions; just get into the limousine."

Sam noticed that her stomach was beginning to hurt as she watched Robert help Danni into the limo. He then smoothed his jacket and stepped inside, leaving Sam to get in on her own. She turned to take one last look at the old apartment building and jumped in.

CHAPTER 6

Sam plopped into her seat.

"Samantha Sue!" Rose said very disapprovingly. "That is not how a lady enters a limousine."

Sam knew she should apologize, but now that she was in the limo, the move felt real! Sam became too excited to contain herself.

"Tell us again, Mom!" she gushed. "How many rooms does the house have? Where is my room? How big is it? I bet it's huge!" Sam held up Olga's cell phone. "You need to warn me when we get close to the house, so I can get in position. See, what I'm going to do is stand up through the sunroof and take a picture of the new house for my blog! Isn't that a great idea? I can't wait to post the first pic—"

"Enough!" Danni covered her ears and snapped, "Mom, tell her to be quiet, she's giving me a headache."

Robert loudly cleared his throat. All three Devines looked at him.

"Ladies, as we leave behind your old home, your old lives, I feel it's worth noting that we have all suffered many trials and tribulations to reach this moment."

Danni and Sam both looked at Robert as though he'd lost his mind, but he continued, "Take in this moment. Remember this day; I promise you, we are on the precipice of an auspicious occasion!"

After a moment of stunned silence, Danni spoke. "Robert, are you okay?"

Rose giggled. Sam thought there was something behind that giggle, something knowing.

"Don't worry about Robert," Rose said with a grin. She turned and spoke directly and rather pointedly to Robert. "Maybe a deep breath and a sip of water would be a good idea."

Sam leaned forward. "One bottled water coming

up!" She turned to grab a bottle from the side compartment and froze! She found herself nose to lens with a video camera in the front seat pointed back at the family.

Sam was so shocked that she didn't move for, like, an entire minute; her brain stopped working. When she finally got it working again, she slowly turned back into her seat.

With her face as white as a ghost, Sam tried to speak softly and without moving her lips, "Don't look now, but there is a video camera in the limo." She thought for a moment and slowly turned her head to focus a steely glower at Robert. "Why is there a video camera in our limo?"

He laughed nervously. "That is part of today's amazing surprise. Let's just sit back and, soon, all will be revealed."

Sam looked at Rose with fear and confusion. Rose smiled and patted her daughter's knee. "Relax, Little Bit. Enjoy the ride."

Sam turned to Danni; she was obviously as confused as Sam was, but didn't seem the slightest bit worried. Danni hummed to herself and twisted her hair around her fingers as she stared absent-mindedly out of a window.

The limo drove off with Sam also looking out of a window, but she wasn't humming or playing with her hair. Sam was trying to get a grip on the intense feeling of dread that had suddenly taken root in her stomach.

It was the longest ten-minute ride of Sam's life.

Finally, the limo pulled up the driveway of the most unbelievably gigantic, glorious, gorgeous estate Sam could have ever dreamed of; she was so amazed that she forgot to stand up through the sunroof and take a picture. The house sat in the middle of a huge half-circled driveway and there were trees all around. Two giant columns stood in front of the stairs that led up to the front door; they reminded Sam of pictures she'd seen of ancient Greek temples. It also reminded her of the home from that old *Beverly Hillbillies* TV show.

The limo stopped directly in front of the columns. As Robert hopped out from the back, a young woman holding that video camera and some guy holding a microphone at the end of a long stick emerged from the front. Robert made a grand gesture of helping Rose and Danni – and even Sam – out of the limo.

He positioned himself directly between the Devine family and their house. "Ladies," he bellowed in a very dramatic voice, "it is my sincere pleasure to be the first to welcome you to your new home! Say hello to Casa Devine!"

Rose was thrilled to see that Danni and Sam both had their jaws open in pleasure and shock! Danni's big blue eyes were about to pop out of her head. She began waving her hands wildly in front of her face to dry her tears of happiness so that her mascara wouldn't run.

Sam began to gush, "It's beautiful! It's so beautiful! It's the most beautiful house in the history of beautiful houses!" She turned to Danni. "And look how big it is! It's so big that you'll be able to snore your head off in one end of the house and I'll barely be able to hear you in the other!"

Danni was so thrilled that she was unable to speak. She was, however, able to give Sam a swift elbow in the gut. After the girls had a minute of pure shock and amazement, Robert grandly lifted his wrist to speak into his wrist-phone.

"Everyone, steady…and…*now*!"

Suddenly, an entire parade marched in from around the back of the house. There was a thirty-piece brass band, about twenty clowns, dozens of acrobats, fire-eaters, and two girls twirling fire batons while carrying a banner that read, "Welcome to Casa Devine." Confetti was flying everywhere. The scene was complete chaos. Robert, Danni, and Rose loved everything about it. They smiled and whooped and waved to everyone marching around. Sam was too stunned to move, but, as usual, nobody was focusing on her.

After the whole parade had circled the driveway, Robert ushered the Devine ladies up the front steps, directly in front of the massive door. He hushed all the parade people and grandly pulled a key out of his pocket.

"Ladies," he again called out dramatically, "I have the unmitigated pleasure of presenting you with the key to your new home!"

Danni proudly took the key. She held it up for the crowd to see. They cheered wildly.

"I can't thank you all enough," she said through her dried tears. "I know that this...this new home, my wonderful career – I know that none of this would be happening if it weren't for you, my wonderful fans!"

The crowd erupted in applause, and it looked as though Danni was going to continue speaking, but Sam jumped in front and yelled out, "But now, it's time for us to move into our new home, so you can all go back to yours. See ya!"

She turned to run into the house, but Robert caught her by the arm.

"Not so fast, Squirt," he hissed in her ear.

Robert pulled four small microphone pins out of his pocket. He spoke out to the crowd as he pinned one on himself, one on Danni, and one on Rose. "As if this day weren't special enough, there's more. Let me introduce you, the Devine family, to two people who are involved in today's surprise and will become an integral part of this wonderful experience."

Robert motioned for the lady with the video camera and the man with the microphone on a stick to come closer. When they did, Robert returned to his loud drama-dude voice. "Ladies, meet your primary camera crew! This is Michi Moto, our video goddess, and Lou Martino, the best boom (that means 'sound guy') in the biz. They will be living in a guesthouse on the back of the property."

Michi and Lou waved unenthusiastically. Danni waved back with a very confused look on her face. Rose turned red; it was pretty obvious that she was upset about something, but was attempting to keep cool in front of the crowd. Sam was deathly still and silent.

After a very uncomfortable minute of everyone standing and staring, Danni turned to Robert and quietly asked, "Um, what's going on here?"

Rose kept a smile on her very red face, but there was genuine anger trembling in her voice. "Living on the property? *Living on the property,* Robert?"

Robert continued announcing as loudly as he could, "You see, Danni, now that you are the planet's number-one pop-singing superstar, the T2CT Network has given you your very own television show!"

Danni squealed with delight. "*Me?* A TV show? *Me?*"

"Yes, my dear." Robert was speaking directly into the camera now. "Recognizing how beloved you are by the entire world, Today's 2 Cool Teens Network has gifted you and your family with this magnificent house in exchange for your participation in your very own reality show!"

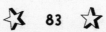

Danni squealed again, "*A TV show?* Me? Oh, this is too much! I just can't believe it! I'm so hap…wait, did you say 'reality show'?"

Robert nodded. "That's the best part. They are going to film your everyday life, the real life of America's number-one pop-star princess! No lines to learn, no costumes, just your real life!"

Rose folded her arms in front of her and glared at Robert with a fierceness that would terrify a tiger. "Living on the property? Twenty-four hours a day? I don't remember that part of the deal, Mr. Ruebens."

Danni had a flash of understanding. "Wait a minute, that means that there will be cameras all over the house, right?"

Robert nodded and showed off those shiny teeth for all they were worth. He was working hard not to make eye contact with Rose in any way.

Danni continued trying to figure out the situation. "Cameras around all the time, huh." She shook her head. "I don't know, Robert. I don't think I like the idea of Planet Earth seeing me when I roll out of bed in the morning."

Robert let out a roaring laugh as if this were the

funniest thing he'd ever heard. "Not that you could ever look bad, my dear, but I know what you mean. That is why your favorite hair and makeup artists, Jean and Jehan Tissaire, will be moving in, as well!"

Robert lifted his arm and snapped his fingers. The front door of the house flew open. Jean and Jehan bounded out of the house, ran over to Danni, gave her a couple of air kisses, stepped back, and stood perfectly still in their most fabulous model-perfect poses.

Danni jumped for joy! "Oh, Robert, you think of everything!" She held the key up and the crowd cheered a little more. Rose closed her eyes, put the back of her hand to her forehead, and spoke to herself in a loud whisper. "I am calm and in control. I am calm and in control." She opened her eyes and glared at Robert with a forced smile.

"Robert," she said in a frighteningly cheerful voice, "I thought we had an understanding about the time and amount of access these people would have to my family. I distinctly remember you agreeing that, while a camera crew would follow us around during the day, they would not be in our faces 24/7. In fact, I know what I signed and nowhere on that contract was there

any mention of other people living in our house. You promised—"

Robert cut her off by putting his arm around her while waving to the crowd.

"Not to worry, Rose," he whispered, "everything will work out. We made a few last-minute changes to the deal, but it's no problem, the crew understands that they can't film everything. Besides, this place is huge! There's plenty of room for everyone."

This comment pushed Sam over the edge from shocked and stunned to completely mental. *Right*, she thought, *plenty of room for everyone whom* Robert *believes is important!* She tugged on Robert's jacket. "What about me?"

He didn't look at her. He just kept waving to the crowd and the cameras. When she wouldn't stop tugging on his expensive Prada jacket, he quietly hissed at Sam out of the side of his mouth, "What *about* you?"

She kept tugging. "Where will *I* live?"

The question surprised Robert enough to get him to look directly at her. "What do you mean? This is your home. You'll live here."

Sam wanted to be sure he understood exactly what

she was saying, so she spoke very slowly. "But if this is Danni's TV show, and this house is filled with cameras, I can't live here."

Robert was completely confused. What was this squirt going on about now? "Look, kid, the show is the real life of Danni Devine – her life, her home, her family."

Sam's eyes narrowed as she glared at Robert with absolute exasperation. "I am not a *kid*. I am twelve years old. Do you seriously *not* know what that means?"

Robert's furrowed eyebrows and clueless expression made it clear to Sam that he had absolutely no idea what she was trying to tell him. She cleared her throat, folded her arms in front of her body, and spoke in her best schoolteacher voice.

"It means, Mr. Ruebens, that I am almost a teenager."

Robert's stare became even more blank and vacant. "Yeah. Sure. Okay."

And with that, Robert moved on with his work. He moved toward Sam to pin the last tiny microphone on her, but she pulled away, stumbling and falling backward up the huge front steps.

"Nope! No. NO WAY!" Sam got back on her feet. "Sorry, but no! I just want a normal life. A normal house and a normal life!"

Danni shot her sister a nasty look. "Zip it, Little Bit!" she loudly whispered. "This isn't about you. It's about *my* life."

Sam thrust her hands on her hips and stared at her sister. "But it's *my* life, too, you know! I want to be normal! Just another normal, dorky twelve-year-old! I don't want to be on TV. I don't like makeup and matching outfits! I don't want camera crews chasing me down the hallway!"

Sam's voice was filled with desperation as she implored her sister, "Come on, Danni! Think about it! You want the whole world to hear you snoring? Take it from me, it's not pretty, you'll lose a whole ton of fans! There'll be letters. You can count on that!"

Rose was torn between wanting to calm her upset daughter and worrying about the publicity of this embarrassing public scene. She reached out to Sam, but Sam pulled back more.

"No!" Sam yelled, putting her hands out to stop anyone from coming closer, "I can't deal with this! I've

waited a whole year for Danni to come home and our family to be normal again! This is the most absolutely awful, no-win, lose-lose mess of my entire life!"

"Honey," Rose said softly with her eyes dancing about at the crowd, "it might be fun. Come on, you don't know if you don't try."

"No, Mom! Not this time. No! No! NO! I'm not going to be some freak in a stupid TV show! I'm going to go to my room and I'm never coming out!"

There was stunned silence from the entire crowd as Sam spun around and ran into the house. For a moment, no one moved a muscle. Then, with her head held high, Sam walked back out with an air of righteous dignity.

"And where would my room be?" she asked.

"Upstairs, second door on your right," Robert replied coolly.

Sam nodded without looking at him. "Thank you."

She twirled around again and marched back into the house. Rose and Danni were too shocked to speak, so, of course, Robert had to say something.

"That may not have been pleasant, but I guarantee the television audience will love it."

 89

CHAPTER 7

Sam found the door to her room and flung it open. What she saw was so shocking, so unbelievably horrifying, that she slumped against the door frame with tears in her eyes. The room was *pink*. Everything in the room was pink. The walls were pink. The carpet was pink. Even the desk in the corner was pink.

She found the strength to walk into the room. Standing in the center, she did a slow turn-around. She nodded as she realized that, yup, every single thing in this freak-show of a bedroom was pink. Sam froze when she saw the gigantic mirror over on the wall. It was the only non-pink thing there; however, written on it, in bright pink lipstick, were the words, "Welcome to your new home, Little Bit!" inside an even brighter pink heart.

Sam slowly walked over to the mirror and glared at the heart. The harder she stared at it, the angrier she became. Her frustration reached a point where she couldn't contain herself; Sam spat on the mirror and rubbed the lipstick with her sleeve, making a big, gooey pink mess. Suddenly, a huge, booming, spooky voice filled the room.

"Please, don't do that!"

Sam jumped back! She looked around. Where had that come from? There was no one in the room except for her. Whatever. She went back up to the mirror and rubbed it again.

"Kid, don't do that!" The loud, spooky voice returned, only this time it sounded annoyed.

At any other time in her life, a disembodied voice would have scared the you-know-what out of Sam, but considering how upset she was with the whole TV show/life as a freak thing, she was too angry to be scared. She yelled back at the voice.

"Don't tell me what to do! You get out of my room,

or my head, or wherever you are!"

There was a moment of silence, and then the voice returned, "Sorry, kid, no can do."

Sam opened her mouth to yell back, but she couldn't think of what to say. What does one say to a loud, ghostly voice booming around one's new bedroom? She sighed a very heavy sigh and threw herself on the bed. Instead of landing on a nice, soft pillow, Sam landed on an ugly, pink doll that let out a loud, "Momma!" Sam leaped off the bed in fear; it took a moment for her to recognize that she'd just squished a stupid toy. She lifted the doll, not sure if she wanted to hurl it or hug it. It was the final straw in a morning that had quickly gone from exciting to rip-roaring disappointing. She plopped down on the floor, put her head in her hands, and began to cry.

"Oh, kid. Don't do that," boomed the voice, a little softer and less fearsome than before.

Sam didn't answer. She kept crying.

The voice sounded almost upset. "Kid, come on. I'm begging you, please don't cry."

Sam raised her head and angrily spat out, "As if you care!"

The voice faltered and stumbled, as if it had no idea how to respond, "It's not…look, this isn't my…I don't, but, aurrrrrrgh!"

Suddenly the mirror slid out and up, like a garage door. Sam could only see a funny blue glare coming from the place where it had been. The voice spoke again, but it was no longer booming all around her; it was coming from what was now a giant hole in Sam's wall.

"Okay, kid. Come here. Let's talk."

Sam's eyes were wide open in astonishment. She leaned forward a bit and was able to see a head full of dreadlocks and two big brown eyes peeking out from inside the blue glare. *Hmmm*, she thought, *either I've snapped and am now seeing things, or there is some dude living inside my bedroom wall; no matter which, this cannot be good.*

Her thoughts were interrupted by the sound of laughter. It was the dreadlocked, brown-eyed, no-longer-spooky-voiced dude, and he was laughing at her!

"What's so funny?" she growled.

Dreadlocked, brown-eyed, no-longer-spooky voiced dude continued laughing. "Oh, kid, the look on your

face. It's priceless." He got his laughing under control. "Look, it's cool. I'm cool. We need to talk, but I can't step outside this room, it's in my contract. Either you come here and we talk, or I'm closing the mirror and going back to my business, and you can sit there and wig out to your heart's content. You make the call."

Before Sam could answer, there was a loud knock at the door.

"Sam?" Rose called out as she jiggled the doorknob. "You okay? Honey? Please unlock the door. I want to talk to you."

Sam let out a frustrated sigh; she was in no mood to deal with her mother. *Oh, why not?* she thought as she jumped up and headed toward the funny blue glare and the dude with the dreads and the big brown eyes. *It's not like things could get that much weirder.*

Sam had to rub her eyes to get them to adjust to the glare and dark light in the little room. Once she could see, she realized that it wasn't such a little room; in fact, it was huge, and it was filled with all kinds of TV screens and electronic equipment.

"Welcome to my brain!" said Mr. Dreadlocks. Sam tried to focus on the TV screens, which were showing all the different rooms in the house and the front- and backyards, but she was really focusing on the guy behind the spooky voice. He didn't look so scary in person. He actually looked kind of cool; no, he looked really cool. He was tall, close to six feet, and was wearing a loose-fitting bowling shirt with a wild orange and red pattern. He looked older than Danni, but younger than Rose, so Sam guessed he was about twenty-nine. His dreadlocks reached his shoulders.

"Are you from Jamaica?" she asked.

He roared with laughter. "What kind of— Why would you ask— You think all black people come from Jamaica?"

Sam was embarrassed by both his laughter and his question. "No! No! I mean because of your hair. I've never seen a person up close with dreadlocks; only on TV, and it was something about Jamaica. I know that not all—" Sam was mortified and frustrated. "I'm not stupid, you know."

He smiled a warm, friendly grin. "I know. Relax, kid. I'm just having a little fun with you."

Sam looked him square in the eye. "I'm so glad you're entertained, but who are you?"

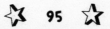

From the corner, there came an enormous gasp! Sam turned her head to discover another person in the room, lurking in the shadows.

"Are you serious?" asked the voice in the shadows. It sounded like a teenage girl, but Sam couldn't see well enough to be sure.

"He's only the biggest director of reality TV on the planet!" The shadow-talker stepped in front of one of the screens and Sam finally saw her. Yup, it was a girl, probably about nineteen years old, wearing a baseball cap that read, *The Devine Life*. "You should be thanking your lucky stars that you got him for your director, 'cause he really is all that and more!"

Sam stared at the girl's baseball cap. *The Devine Life?* What is *that*? Then it hit Sam…that must be the name of Danni's TV show! That's what this is! These people are working on the television show! Sam ignored the girl and turned her attention back to Mr. Dreadlocks.

"If you're such a big shot, then why are you living inside my wall?"

Sam could see he wanted to laugh again, but he held it in. "Blame your mother, kid," he said. "She visited the house yesterday and demanded that you get that room out there. It was supposed to be your mom's private office, so me working in here wouldn't have been a big deal, but she made her decision and I was stuck because all my equipment was already in place."

Sam glared at him. "Well, I guess you'll just have to move all your equipment, won't you?"

Mr. Dreadlocks stayed unemotional. "I'm directing your sister's TV show. I need a central location for what I call my brain, my control room, where I can sit with all my monitors and watch what goes on in all the different areas of this house. This room is central and it's hidden, which makes it perfect for me. If you don't like it, then you can move, but I'm not going anywhere."

Sam glared at him with even more intensity. "And where am I supposed to go?"

He ignored the snottiness in her tone and walked over to a wall with several screens showing different rooms in the house. "I don't really care, but take a look." He pointed at some screens that showed bedrooms. "This house has about ten bedrooms. I'm sure you can find one you'll like."

Sam stood her ground. "I'm not talking about finding a room I'd like, I'm talking about the fact that I don't like any of this! I don't want to be on TV!"

Another loud gasp came from Baseball-Cap Girl. "Stop it!" she sneered at Sam. "Everybody wants to be on TV!"

The energy in the room turned ugly. Mr. Dreadlocks jumped in before it got even uglier. He pointed to Baseball-Cap Girl, "You, out!" Then, he pointed to Sam, "You, sit!"

Baseball-Cap Girl opened her mouth to argue, but she caught herself. She threw a nasty look at Sam and sulked down a trapdoor in the floor. Sam sat in the nearest chair. Mr. Dreadlocks sat on a bench across from Sam and waited for her to speak.

When she finally did, Sam's voice had a ring of desperation in it, "Listen, Mr...."

"Bluford, Malcolm Bluford." He extended his hand. "Call me Blu."

Sam didn't shake his hand; she kept hers tightly folded in front of her. "Okay, Blu. Here's the situation, either you go or I will."

Blu took a deep breath before answering. "Kid, I can

see you're upset about all this, but you have to stay. If you don't do the show, it's over."

Sam snorted. "Yeah, right."

Blu wasn't smiling. "I'm dead serious."

Sam threw open her arms. "Why? Who cares about me? Nobody even knows I'm alive!"

Blu's voice became soft and gentle. "Your family does."

Sam snorted again and looked down with tears in her eyes.

Blu saw that the situation was pretty painful for the poor kid. "Hey, *I* know you're alive. Look, the only reason I agreed to direct this show was because of you, what it's like for a normal kid to live with all this superstar-sister craziness. That's the story here, your reality, not your sister's, not your mom's — *your* reality!"

Sam looked up at Blu. Big, fat tears welled up in her eyes. "No," she spluttered, "not my reality! Go pick on someone else's reality! Leave me alone!"

Blu clearly hadn't expected the kid to completely melt down like this. He'd seen her temper tantrum outside via one of the television monitors, but having

her cry in front of him was more than he could take. He seemed genuinely upset about how bad this little girl seemed to be feeling. He looked around for a tissue, but there wasn't any.

"Shhh, calm down, calm down," he urged Sam as he continued to scour the room for anything she could use to dry her eyes. "Don't cry. We'll figure something out, but you have to calm down. Come on, kid, breathe."

That was it! The tears spilled down Sam's cheeks as she cried out, "Quit calling me 'kid'! I'm not a little kid! I'm twelve! How come nobody gets it? Don't you understand what that means?"

"Umm," Blu recognized that this was a make-or-break moment. The kid, the girl, was sincerely upset, and if he said the wrong thing, then she might completely wig out and the situation would be unsalvageable. He forced a grin on his face and replied in a voice filled with gentle understanding and a little optimism, "It means you're almost thirteen?"

"It means I'm..." Sam caught herself. Had she heard what she thought she'd heard? Was this guy actually listening to her? She looked up at Blu in amazement. He really was listening to her! She wiped a few of her tears away and stared at him intently, trying to figure out if he was being nice or making fun of her. "That's right," she said slowly. "It means I'm almost a teenager and not a little kid."

Blu nodded and looked around again for anything the girl could use to wipe her eyes, but there was absolutely nothing, so he stood up and offered her the corner of his shirt. For a moment she stared at him as if he were completely insane; then she cracked a tiny smile. This broke the tension in the room enough for Blu to sit back down and try to find some way to work through this whole rotten mess.

"Okay, I tell you what, we'll make a deal, you and me, but you have to take it seriously. If you are completely, one hundred percent, sick-to-your-stomach, unable to be in this show, then I'll quit. And if I quit, there is no show because," Blu's tone and pitch changed so that he sounded exactly like Baseball-Cap Girl, "I am the top reality TV director!" He smiled and continued in his normal voice, "I really am, you know, and if I quit the show, then it's over. The network won't pay to produce the show without me.

So here's the deal. Give me five days, a measly five little days; that's how long it takes me to produce an episode. During that time, you go about your life, do the things you normally do, and see how it goes. Be sure you take some time to really think about all this. On that fifth day, I'll let you see the show I've put together; then, if you still say 'no', I'll quit, and you'll be free."

Sam was stunned. She stared at Blu with her mouth agape. It took her a full minute to find her voice. "You mean it? You won't do the show without me? You think I'm that important?"

Blu smiled. "Of course I do. Plus, listen, I grew up with four older sisters. I know what it's like to get your life completely trampled on by an older sibling. It's a cruddy situation and there's not a thing you can do about it, usually. Here's one time where you can be the one who gets to make the decision."

Blu extended his hand again. "Okay?"

Sam looked at him suspiciously. "For real?"

Blu kept his hand extended and smiled. "For real. You have my word. It's you or nothing, kid – whoops." Blu slapped both hands over his mouth. "Sorry. Sorry. Sorry." He kept one hand over his mouth and

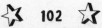

re-extended the other for Sam to shake. "Let's try that again. It's you or nothing. Deal?"

Sam's hand slowly rose, but she pulled it back. "Hang on, I can't believe I'm hearing this. You'd give up all the money they're paying you, you'll pack up and go home, for *me*? You'd really do that?"

With a very serious, but sincere, look, Blu stared into Sam's eyes. "No offense, but you and your family aren't the only game in town. Life is too short, and there are too many other opportunities for me out there to spend my time on a job that would be a miserable experience. I'd rather bail on this gig and do something that would be enjoyable than sit around and fight with you day and night. Besides, you know how this whole fame thing works, don't you? In three weeks there will be someone else the whole world is in love with and your sister will be old news. First the TV shows and magazines talk about you like you're the greatest thing in the world, then they decide their audience is bored so they start writing stories about you no longer being the hottest thing, and suddenly, you are 'so yesterday'. Don't think you're doing me any big favor by sticking this out. If you decide to do it, do it for yourself and your family, not for me or anyone else."

Sam smiled, stood, and began to stretch out her hand, but one last issue popped into her head. She froze, her entire body as still as a statue, about six inches away from Blu. "Today counts, right?"

"Huh?" Blu cocked his head to the side, the way a puppy does when its master gives a command it doesn't understand. "Today, what?"

Sam took in a deep breath and stretched herself to look as tall as possible. She had to iron out this last important item before agreeing to any deal. "Today counts as day number one. It's still morning, so I believe that today should be counted as the first day of our five-day agreement."

Blu had to bite the corners of his mouth to stop the giant grin that wanted to spread across his face. He seemed both amused and impressed with the seriousness and maturity of these negotiations. *This was no ordinary kid, err...pre-teenager,* he thought.

"You drive a very hard bargain, Miss Devine, but yes, today will count as day number one. I can agree to these terms."

Sam was so pleasantly surprised that the negotiation had worked out so well that she said out loud, "Huh, we found a win-win outcome. This stuff really works!"

Blu snorted. "Who do you think you are? Donald Trump?"

Blu's comments snapped Sam back into the seriousness of the moment. She realized it was time to shake hands and cement the deal. She stretched out her hand all the way, but yanked it back as quickly as she could.

Blu let out an aggravated sigh. "Now what's the problem?"

Sam looked down as she searched for the best way to discuss a downright embarrassing detail. "You don't have cameras in the bathroom, do you?"

There was pure amusement in Blu's voice. "I get it. You're trying to ask if I'll get you on videotape on the toilet or in the shower?"

Sam snapped back, "It's a fair question!"

This time Blu's voice was full of understanding. "You don't need to worry, the bathroom mirrors and cameras are all placed so it's impossible for me to see anything you wouldn't want anyone to see. And, in

case you are wondering, I'm not some Peeping Tom. Remember the girl who was in here earlier, the production assistant in the baseball cap? My contract states that there will always be a female assistant in here with me and her only job is to cut the feed from any camera when someone changes clothes or anything like that. I promise, you don't need to worry."

Sam took one last moment to try to read Blu's face to be sure she wasn't being tricked or lied to about any of this stuff. She decided that he was being honest and was worth trusting. She nodded as she forcefully stuck her hand out and proclaimed, "My name is Samantha Sue Devine. You can call me Sam, and Mr. Blu, you have got yourself a deal."

They shook on it and not another word was said. Sam turned and left the room. Blu shook his head in admiration and disbelief at how such a little girl had gotten him to make such a major deal. He lowered the mirror door as Sam stepped back into the pink nightmare.

Alone in her room, Sam took another long look at her surroundings. *It would be funny if it weren't so awful,* she thought. With one last, deep, anguished

sigh, Sam headed to the corner where her boxes and suitcases had been piled up. She opened the box marked "Sam's Stuff! Important Posters – Don't Even Think About Touching" written in big red letters. She pulled out one of her many horse posters, and tacked it onto the wall.

"Well, it's a start. Only about a hundred to go and I shouldn't be able to see anymore of the pink on the walls." She giggled at herself and made a mental note to put that in her blog entry later that evening.

Suddenly Sam got a flash of a thought. She turned and pounded on the huge mirror.

"Hey, Blu!" she shouted out.

Blu's booming voice filled the room. "You don't have to beat up the mirror to get my attention. I can see you, remember?"

She stopped pounding. "Oh, yeah. Hey! Tell me again why I got stuck with this pukey pink room? There has to be a reason. My mom wouldn't do this to me unless there was a real reason."

"It's like I told you, ki— Sam. I'm not sure." Blu tried to remember exactly what had happened. "Let's see, your mother came in yesterday. She walked in, looked around, and said she didn't care what it took or how much stuff we had to switch around, but you had to have this room. I don't know, maybe something over by the window?"

"The window?" Sam wondered as she walked over to the big, wide window by her computer desk. She looked out and saw the backyard, the swimming pool, a couple of neighbors' backyards, and – OH! Stunned, Sam was absolutely stunned and speechless! Suddenly she erupted into a loud, crazy victory dance. She was bouncing and yelling and making a joyful, squeaky noise. The doorknob jiggled. The door rattled. The doorknob jiggled again and Rose, Danni, and Robert all burst into the room. Rose held the key in her hand and was shaking so hard that Robert took it away from her before she dropped it. Of course, Rose, Danni, and Robert were followed by Michi and Lou doing their camera crew stuff.

Rose grabbed Sam by the shoulders and looked at her with pure worry in her eyes. "Sam? You all right, honey? Please tell me you're all right!"

Sam jumped into Rose's arms and hugged her with all her might.

"Thank you, Mom! Thank you, Mom! Thank you, Mom!" she gushed.

Rose grinned from ear to ear. "You finally looked out the window?"

Sam was so overcome with happiness that she couldn't speak. She nodded while still clinging to Rose.

Rose chuckled and smoothed Sam's hair. "Yeah, I may miss a few things, but your old mom always tries."

Danni and Robert both stared at the scene with pure confusion.

"What's the big deal?" Danni asked as she headed toward the window. "What could be so..." Danni looked out. "Oh, I see."

Robert and the camera crew joined Danni at the window.

"What," Robert asked Danni with annoyance oozing from his voice, "is the cause of this touching family moment?"

Danni smiled and pointed out the window.

"Right there, Robert. Don't you see it, the big sign with the green letters? The one that reads 'SuAn Stables'?"

Robert gave Danni a "so what" look. "And?"

Danni put her hands on her hips and stared directly into her agent's eyes. She spoke in the kind of steely, calm voice that Rose used whenever she was frighteningly serious about something.

"And, Robert," Danni said with a stern smile on her lips, "my little sister is hard-core crazy for that place, and now that she realizes her bedroom is spitting distance from her beloved horsies, she may mellow out about this whole TV thing."

Robert nodded to Danni. He got it.

He turned to the camera and flashed his fabulous smile. "That's right!" he cooed. "Everything works out for everyone when you live THE DEVINE LIFE!"

Everyone in the room, even the camera crew, groaned and rolled their eyes in disgust.

CHAPTER 8

Click click click, clack clack click.

I'm sitting in the middle of the carpet that's in the middle of my new room that's in the middle of my new house…which means I'm smack in the middle of my sister's stinky TV show. (sigh)

Mom hustled Robert and Danni and the camera crew out of my room so that I could have time to myself, as if a little "alone time" would convince me that being trapped in a reality TV show was a good thing. HA!

I don't get it. I woke up this morning the happiest girl in the whole world — my sister was back home, we were moving into a first family house — and now I'm so mixed up, I'm close to barfing my guts out. Why did I agree to this cruddy situation? That Blu is a very tricky guy. I'm going to have to watch him. He seemed so genuine that I found myself agreeing to his "give me five days" agreement before I really thought it through. Five days. That's a whole week in school days. 120 hours of somebody videotaping everything I do, say, eat, and think (well — they can't videotape what I think, can they??? I hope not!!). (deep sigh)

I need to talk to my mom. I can't believe she said yes to this freak-show life. What was she thinking? *Was* she thinking??

Okay, that was kind of snotty. Could I be coming down too hard on Mom? After all, she did get us a house a stone's throw from the stables and then she made sure that I got the room that has

 112

the great big, beautiful view of the stables. My stables! That is the one saving grace of this nightmare. We are close enough that I can actually see the people riding in the center ring!

Do I need to lighten up? Maybe Mom really did have a good reason for agreeing to this stupid reality show. That must be it; there must be some brilliant reason, some important thing that made Mom believe this WAS a good idea. I need to talk to her – but not now – later – maybe.

It was about three hours after her meltdown on the front steps that Sam sneaked out of her room, down the stairs, and into the garage. She found her bike and quietly walked it around to the front of the house. She was about to ride off when Danni walked over to her. Sam hung her head and took a deep breath; she had no idea what Danni was going to say to her or what she was going to say to Danni. Seeing as Rose had hustled everybody out of Sam's room before the girls had had a chance to talk, neither sister quite knew what to say to the other.

There was a very uncomfortable minute where no one spoke but, finally, Danni asked, "What are you doing?"

Sam's first reaction was to snap back with a snarky comment, but she saw that her sister was trying to make peace, so she quietly answered, "Thought I'd go for a ride, visit the stables, and get Mom some flowers. I feel bad about freaking out like I did…in front of all those people, I mean."

Danni was both surprised and impressed. "Wow. Good thinking, Little Bit. Got any money?"

Sam nodded, "Some," and held up a bag of quarters.

Danni bit her lower lip to stop herself from laughing at the pathetically cute sight of her kid sister holding up a bag of change to buy something for Mommy. "Here." She dug into a pocket and pulled out a wad of cash. "Get Mom something nice."

Sam was shocked! Where had Danni gotten all that money? Danni waited for Sam to take it. When she didn't, Danni reached out, grabbed Sam's left hand, and slapped the wad of bills into it. The wad was so big that Sam's hand could barely close around it.

Danni caught sight of Robert peeking at them from the window. She saw him barking something into his wrist-phone, but keeping both eyes on the girls. "Oh, boy. Sam?" She suddenly seemed very worried. "You'd better move it, Little Bit. You've probably got about ten seconds before—"

Suddenly a Jeep roared around from behind the house and pulled up next to the girls.

Danni hung her head and completed her warning, "…before the camera crew finds you."

Robert walked out, smiling at the people in the Jeep. "Ahh, beautiful day for a little bike ride, don't you think, folks?" He turned to Sam. "Your mother will be pleased to see you out of your room."

Sam was confused. "What's going on here?"

Danni was afraid Sam was about to have another massive temper tantrum. She put her face in her hands and held her breath.

Robert pointed to the Jeep. "They go," he pointed back at Sam, "wherever you go."

Sam looked so surprised that Robert almost laughed. "Oh, don't worry," he said. "You won't even know they're there."

Sam realized that the people in the Jeep were Michi and Lou, and they were videotaping her! She shot Danni a look of desperation. Peeking through her fingers, Danni smiled weakly.

"Go on, Sam," she urged. "It won't be that bad."

Sam grimaced, shoved the wad of money in her pocket, and rode off, trying unsuccessfully to forget that she was being followed and videotaped.

"Oh, man," she muttered, "this is so not my reality."

Sam rode a few blocks until she reached a stop sign. She needed a minute to get her bearings and decide which street to take to get to the stables from this location. The Jeep with the camera crew stayed behind her, taping her standing still.

"This must be very exciting for you!" Sam yelled back at the Jeep, "taping me thinking. Wow! How thrilling."

Michi kept her eye glued to the camera's eyepiece, but raised her right hand and gave Sam a big thumbs up. Sam couldn't tell if that meant Michi knew she was being sarcastic, or she was trying to tell Sam that the taping was going well.

Just as Sam decided to go to the left, a car drove up beside her. The back window rolled down and two girls about Sam's age popped their heads out.

"You!" one girl yelled at Sam. "You! I saw you on TV last night! You're the sister! I love Danni! Where is she?"

The other girl chimed in, "Yeah! Where's Danni?"

"Um." Sam was so surprised she needed a second to find her voice. "She, she's back at home."

From the front seat, the mother yelled out, "Who are you talking to?"

"It's Danni Devine's sister," Sam heard the first girl say.

"Just the sister? She's a nobody," snapped the mom. "I don't have time for this."

The car drove off, leaving Sam standing at the stop sign, holding her bike, and feeling both confused and hurt.

Right, it's nobody, she thought to herself. She turned and yelled back at the camera crew, "Did you get that?"

This time it was Lou, still holding the microphone on the end of a long stick, who gave Sam a thumbs up.

117

Michi, still with her eye glued to the camera's eyepiece, nodded, but from Sam's perspective it looked as if the video camera were nodding at her. She shook her head in disbelief at the bizarreness of it all and rode off.

As she reached the driveway of the SuAn Stables, Sam took a deep breath and said a silent prayer that Mr. Wattabee, the manager, wouldn't be working in the security-guard booth. He'd been consistently rude and dismissive to Sam since the day she'd begun working there. She'd never understood exactly what it was about her that he found so distasteful, but she guessed that it had to do with his inflated idea of himself as the protector of all the wealthy patrons who paid a ton of money to ride at the stables. He imagined that he had to keep them well segregated from the grunts, like Sam, who worked there and might contaminate their exalted status. That was why she and Olga secretly called him Mr. *Wannabee*; he so obviously *wanted to be* some rich, important guy. That name, Wannabee, fit him so well that Sam had to sometimes bite her tongue from accidentally calling him that to his face.

Sam didn't see anyone in the guard booth at the entrance. She sighed with relief as she flattened herself down onto her bike to ride under the large red and white security rail blocking the entryway. Unfortunately, just as her head was clearing the rail, someone angrily called out her name. This spooked her; she jumped a tiny bit, but that tiny bit was enough to slam her head into the rail. She fell off her bike and lay sprawled out in the middle of the driveway.

Mr. Wattabee waddled over to her. Sam looked up to see his puffy red face glaring down at her.

"Trying to sneak in without signing in, Devine?" he growled.

Sam struggled to raise herself up to a sitting position, rubbed her head, and woozily answered, "No, sir. I mean, yes, sir, I was…I…" She couldn't get her thoughts straight because her head was starting to throb.

A honk from the Jeep startled both Sam and Mr. Wattabee. Lou yelled out, "Hey, Buddy, you wanna lift that barrier so we can come in? We're with Sam."

Mr. Wattabee opened his mouth to argue, but froze when he saw the video camera pointed directly at him.

He looked back and forth from Sam to the camera several times before slowly turning so that only his back was being taped.

"What's going on here, Devine?" he whispered.

"It's my sister's TV show," Sam explained as she blinked her eyes over and over to try to get them to focus. "My family's been sucked into this reality thing because of my sister."

Mr. Wattabee tried to be nonchalant as he peeked over his shoulder to see if the cameras were still trained on him. "Your sister?" he asked. "I didn't know you had a sister. Who is she?"

Still not looking at him, Sam answered, "Danni."

Mr. Wattabee drew in a sharp breath. "Danni Devine? You're *Danni Devine's* sister?" His head was moving back and forth from the camera to Sam so quickly it looked in danger of popping off.

Sam nodded gingerly as the pain behind her eyes began to fade. She shook her head one last time to clear away the final remnants of the sting and was rolling over onto her side to stand up when suddenly she was lifted into the air. Mr. Wattabee had grabbed her arm and hoisted her up to a standing position. Sam wasn't

prepared for this; she was so wobbly, she almost fell over again.

"Whoa there, Little Filly," he said as he helped Sam steady herself. "You need to take it easy till you get your legs back underneath you."

Sam squinted her eyes and stared at him. "What?"

Something strange began to happen to Mr. Wattabee's face. Sam had only ever seen it frowning or scowling, but it appeared to be moving into a shape she was unfamiliar with, a shape that, dare she believe her eyes, looked almost like a smile.

"I said," Mr. Wattabee bellowed in a totally unnaturally loud and cheerful voice, "you need to take it easy for a bit. You took quite a bump to your forehead. We need to be certain you didn't do any real damage to that pretty little head of yours."

A display of caring from Mr. Wattabee was more than just bizarre, it was utterly unheard of, it was so unimaginable that the only thing Sam could figure out was that she'd smacked her skull so hard she was seeing things that weren't really there. Yeah, that had to be it, that bonk on her bean must have scrambled her brain.

Michi, keeping her camera rolling, called out, "Samantha, Blu is yelling into my earpiece. He wants to know if we need to call your mom or an ambulance."

Suddenly Sam remembered the whole stinky situation. Not only had she just stacked it on her bike in front of the stables, she'd done it while being videotaped.

"No, Michi," she replied with an obvious touch of sad acceptance in her voice, "I'm okay. The only thing I hurt was my ego."

Mr. Wattabee swung an arm around and slapped Sam hard on the back. "She's a tough one, our Sammy," he roared toward the camera. "Yes-siree, that's what we all say around here, our Sammy is one feisty little bronco."

Again Sam stared up at Mr. Wattabee in confusion. What was going on here? Why was he acting as if she were his bestest buddy? For the past four years, the man had never so much as offered her a kind nod of the head. Every time Sam had smiled or said hello to him, he'd either ignored her or grunted about something she'd done wrong (like not signing in or not signing out – the kind of unimportant stuff adults like to turn into a major big deal).

Mr. Wattabee spoke again in that freaky loud voice he'd been using since lifting Sam up off the ground. "Miss Devine, how long will these fine folks be following you around with that fancy videotaping machine?"

"Don't know," she replied while taking note of the fact that Mr. Wattabee's eyes were firmly fixed on the camera, even while he was talking to her. "At least the next five days."

Mr. Wattabee jumped with excitement. "Five days?" He ran as fast as his chubby legs could back to the guard booth, grabbed something, and hustled back to Sam, but when he spoke, it was, again, directly into the camera. "I bet you didn't know, Sammy, that old Mr. Wattabee here is the lead tenor in our local light opera company!"

"No, sir," Sam replied, looking back and forth from the camera to Mr. Wattabee's flushed face, "I didn't know that."

"It's true! I, Mr. Phinneas T. Wattabee, am one heck of a singer, and this Sunday, I am starring in our wonderful little production of the Lerner and Loewe

classic musical, *My Fair Lady*! Not to brag, but since we are on the subject, I'll share with you that I, Mr. Phinneas T. Wattabee, am playing the lead character!"

"The lead character?" Sam asked. "You're the *fair lady*?"

Mr. Wattabee looked at Sam. He took a moment to assess if she truly didn't understand or if she was making fun of him. He quickly deduced that she was being genuine – ignorant, but genuine. He let out a guffaw that was too darn loud and way too cheerful to be real.

"That was very funny, Sammy! Very funny, indeed! No, my girl, I am playing the lead male character, the brilliant Professor Henry Higgins!"

Sam opened her mouth to speak, but before she could, Mr. Wattabee thrust his arms toward the camera and began singing. "The rain in Spain falls mainly on the plain."

His singing was so loud that not only Sam, but even Lou and Michi, still in the Jeep, flinched. Sam looked around and noticed that people up at the stables were staring in her direction, trying to figure out where that awful warbling was coming from.

"Mr. Wan— I mean, Mr. Wattabee?" Sam asked, in the hope of getting him to be quiet.

"The rain in Spain falls mainly on the plain," he continued singing, oblivious to the crowd that was slowly headed his way.

"Please, sir," Sam implored, as she saw more and more people walking toward the guard booth.

Stepping closer to the camera, the chubby, red-faced Mr. Wattabee whipped his arms about as if he were directing an imaginary orchestra, singing with even more gusto, "And where is that soggy plain?"

The crowd was very close now and Sam was desperate to stop the situation before it completely deteriorated and she became the absolute laughing stock of the stable. She threw herself in front of Mr. Wattabee and began clapping wildly.

"That was great! Wow! Awesome! Totally, wickedly, unbelievably, out-of-control awesome!" Sam frantically bounced around to draw Mr. Wattabee's attention away from the camera. "Honestly, I'd love to hear you do that again sometime!"

That got his attention. He stopped singing and proudly held out four tickets. "Wonderful! Then you'll

125

come to the show? It's this Sunday. You and your sister will love it!" He turned to speak to Michi and Lou. "Of course I understand you two will be tagging along. Know that you are most welcome! I'm proud to share my gift of song with all my fellows in…" He pulled his arms in so that his hands were directly in front of his face, held up the two first fingers on each hand, and made air quotations, "… 'the biz'."

Sam was so relieved to have gotten him to stop singing that she missed her opportunity to escape and asked, "What biz?"

Focusing again into the camera, Mr. Wattabee let out a thunderous "Ho ho ho," sounding more like a demented Santa Claus than a normal human being, and said, "The biz! *Show*biz! You know," he began singing again, "the one business that's like no business I know!"

Sam couldn't take anymore weirdness. She lunged at Mr. Wattabee and grabbed the tickets from his hand. "Great! Got it," she yelled to cut him off from continuing. "I'll be there! I promise! Okay? I'll be there!"

Grinning from ear to ear, Mr. Wattabee patted (more like slammed) Sam on the back again. "Wonderful!

Wonderful! I look forward to sharing my talent with you and your television family."

Sam raced back to pick up her bike. "Super. Can't wait." She walked her bike around the security pole, toward the street.

"Sammy," Mr. Wattabee called out. "I thought you were coming in for a ride!"

Sam shook her head. "Changed my mind. I just want to go home."

By now, six cars were lined up behind the Jeep, waiting to get into the stables. The driver of the lead car began to honk in annoyance.

Mr. Wattabee immediately returned to his normal state of grumpiness and scowled at the driver. "One minute!" He turned back to Sam, his freaky friendly persona reemerging. "All right, my dear. Have a great day! Look forward to seeing you at the show!"

Another honk, this one longer and seemingly angrier, blared from the car. Mr. Wattabee spun on his heels and glared at the driver. Sam took the opportunity to jump on her bike and pedal away as fast as she could. As she did, she heard Mr. Wattabee yelling out, "And be sure to tell your sister I said hello."

Sam shook her head and zoomed down the street. Her brain was spinning as she tried to make sense of the total weirdness she'd just escaped. She was so deep in thought, she didn't even realize she was talking out loud. "'Tell your sister I said hello'? *Tell your sister I said hello?* What was that all about? He doesn't even know Danni! He didn't even know I had a sister!"

Sam rode up to a traffic signal that was just turning red. She stopped, but her focus was still on trying to understand Mr. Wattabee's bizarre behavior. She looked at the tickets in her hand and remembered his horrible warbling at the top of his lungs. "Ewwww." She tried to block the memory, but his horrific voice had wrapped itself around her brain. She hung her head, closed her eyes, put her hands over her ears, and attempted to cancel out Mr. Wattabee's voice with her own by loudly singing the first song she could think of. "A, b, c, d, e, f, g."

By the time she reached, "w," Sam opened her eyes. She noticed tires next to her. Her voiced trailed off as she looked up to see Michi's video camera right in her face.

Sam swallowed the lump in her throat and asked,

"How long have you been filming me?"

Lou's voice was neutral, but he was fighting not to let the corners of his mouth lift into a grin as he replied, "We caught up with you around the letter 'p'."

Sam's hands moved from her ears to her eyes. Could this day get any worse? She lifted her head, took in a deep breath, dropped her hands down to her side, stared into the camera, and let out a slow, wet raspberry.

Michi and Lou were so caught off guard at this that they both laughed. This reaction surprised Sam, but it bolstered her spirit. She shot a sly, little grin at the Jeep as she took off on her bike in search of a place to buy some flowers for her mother.

After a good fifteen minutes of riding around the neighborhood, Sam found a small flower shop and turned into the empty parking lot. The Jeep pulled up next to her, so Sam leaned her bike against it.

"You wait here," she said to the crew. "I'm just going in for a minute."

Michi, with her eye still glued to the camera's eyepiece, began to climb out of the Jeep, but Sam yelled out at her, "Stay! I mean it! I'll be right out. You stay here!"

Michi settled back into the Jeep as Sam entered the shop. The crew kept taping. Even though the only thing visible through the lens was the closed front door of the shop, Sam's microphone was picking up all the noise inside.

Sam took in a big, sweet smell of all the different flowers as she closed the door behind her. A smiling woman wearing a bright green apron walked over to her.

"Welcome to Frida's Flowers. Can I help you?"

"Yes, please. I'd like a dozen—"

The florist cut her off. "Wait a minute. I know you. You used to come into my old shop, over on the other side of town. You were the girl who always had those bags of quarters! Haven't seen you in while. Back to get more carnations for your mother?"

Sam grinned. "Yup! Today is a very special day and I would like a dozen—"

The florist cut her off again, turning to go into the giant cooler. "That's so sweet. I'll get your carnations."

"Not carnations today, ma'am." Sam reached out to stop the florist. "I'm here to get a real bouquet! I would like a dozen roses!"

The florist turned back to face Sam rather slowly. Her eyebrows were arched and her voice had a snippy edge. "Oh, so all those bunches of carnations I put together for you before...those weren't *real* bouquets?"

The edge in the florist's voice surprised Sam. She stumbled back a bit. "I didn't mean that. It's just, well, now I can pay for something special, so—"

Not only did the florist cut Sam off again, she took a menacing step forward. "Young lady," she growled, "my birthday is December 23rd. That makes me a Capricorn. I'm a stickler for justice and doing the right thing. My birthstone is the garnet, and my birth flower is the carnation, but hey, if that's not good enough for you, then fine. I'll be right out with your dozen roses. I hope you recognize that you won't be able to pay for this bouquet with a bag of quarters."

Sam's face turned bright red. She was completely confused. Her mouth opened, but no words came out. There was a moment of total, awkward, uncomfortable energy. The silence was broken by a high-pitched squeal.

"The sister! The sister!"

A teenage girl came running into the room. She was wearing the same kind of green apron as the florist.

"Mother!" gushed the girl. "It's the sister! It's the sister!"

The florist turned to the girl with a face that made it clear she had no idea what all the commotion was about.

"Danni Devine! This is Danni Devine's sister!" The girl couldn't believe her mother didn't understand how huge this was. "Remember last night when I was laughing so hard you thought I was going to wet my pants? Remember?"

The florist nodded. "Yes?"

"This is her!" the girl continued. "This is the kid who burped on TV!"

Sam cringed, but the girl kept on squealing. "I just love Danni! I think your sister is a total goddess! She is the most amazing singer on the planet! Is she here? Where is she? Is she here? I can't believe this! I'm standing here with Danni Devine's little sister! I love her CD! I listen to it all the time!"

The florist turned back to Sam with a snarl on her lips.

132

"Ah," she said, as if she'd just solved some big mystery. "So that's why you're suddenly too good for carnations."

Sam tried to tell her that this wasn't the way it seemed, but the florist turned her head and kept talking.

"No problem. I'll go get your special bouquet. Just a moment, please."

Before the florist could leave the room, her daughter jumped on her.

"Oh, Mother, let me make it, please? Please, Mother? *Please?* Nothing could be better than for me to make a bouquet for Danni Devine!"

"Umm...actually, it's for our mom," Sam explained in a pathetically little voice.

The florist's daughter continued jumping around the room.

"Whatever! The point is that Danni will see it and love it and want to get all her flowers here, and we'll become best friends and hang out and it'll be the best thing ever!"

The girl made one last grand jump and landed almost on top of Sam. She grabbed Sam by the shoulders and looked directly into her eyes.

"Don't move!" she shouted in Sam's face.

The girl vanished into the back room, leaving Sam alone with the florist. No one spoke. Sam could feel the florist staring at her with pure disdain. Sam wanted to explain that this was all just a misunderstanding, she didn't think there was anything wrong with carnations and it wasn't her money she was using to buy the roses, but she couldn't speak.

Finally, the florist's daughter ran back into the room carrying the biggest, most grotesque, and just plain dumb-looking bouquet in the history of flowers. Sam's eyes almost popped out of her head.

"Wow," was what came out of Sam's mouth, when what she was really thinking was: *that has to be the ugliest bunch of flowers in the entire universe.*

"Here you go!" beamed the girl. "I hope Danni loves it! I used all the most colorful flowers! I just know somebody as famous and talented as her must be a very colorful person. Do you think she'll like it? Do you?"

Sam took a deep breath and replied, "I'm sure she'll never forget it," as she reached into her pocket (which was a major struggle with that massive bunch of flowers in her arms) and pulled out the wad of cash.

"What do I owe you, please?" she asked without making eye contact with the nasty florist lady.

"Oh, no!" The florist's daughter shook her head violently. "This is on the house! We would never dream of taking money from Danni Devine!"

Sam didn't understand. "Umm…no, really, how much do I owe you?"

The girl gave her mother a look that implored her to help. The florist gave Sam a nasty smile. "Like my daughter said, this bouquet is on the house. Just remember us next time you want flowers. We deliver anywhere."

"But…but…" Sam stammered in confusion. "But I have the money."

The florist walked over to the door and waited for Sam to follow.

"Keep your money," she said. "Consider this a gift from Frida's Flowers."

Sam had no idea what was going on. She shook her head in disbelief.

"I don't get it. When I didn't have any money, you took my quarters. Now I have lots of money, and you're giving me flowers for free?"

The florist drew in a sharp breath. Sam thought the woman was going to reach out and throttle her, but the woman kept both hands down by her sides.

"Young lady," the florist hissed, "I will thank you not to brag in my store!"

"That's not what I...I didn't mean to..." Sam was too freaked out by the whole scene to get a single thought out. "I'm sorry...I...thank you. Thank you both very much."

Sam leaned against the flower-shop door to get out of there as fast as she could. As she stepped outside, the bright light blinded her for a second, but her ears were still working. She heard snippets of whispering.

"Is it...?"

"Is she...?"

"I don't know."

When Sam's eyes adjusted to the sunlight, she saw that she was completely surrounded by a crowd of kids and teenagers. They were everywhere; they completely filled the parking lot. They'd even surrounded the Jeep. They were whispering to each other, looking at the camera, and waiting for something. Unfortunately, that something had just come outside.

From the middle of the crowd, the two girls whose mother had totally dismissed Sam at the stop sign ten minutes earlier, pointed and yelled out, "There she is! That's her! That's the sister!"

Sam was ambushed. Light bulbs flashed, people were shoving pens and autograph books in her face, and squealing in her ears, "Where is Danni? I love Danni!"

Sam struggled to get to her bike. By the time she reached it, the flowers were completely trashed. She shoved them into her basket and tried to hop on her bike. As she swung a leg over, she kicked the side of the Jeep. It hurt so badly her eyes began to fill with tears.

Sam looked up and saw that the camera was directly in her face. She glared and screamed into the lens, "Blu! Hey, Blu! Yeah, I'm talking to you, Mister Bluford! I know you're watching this. I dare you to ask me again why I don't want to do this stupid show! I double-dare you!"

CHAPTER 9

Click click click, clack clack click.

Day #1 of my agreement with Blu has finally become night (I'm supposed to be sleeping already). I am seriously thinking about writing a letter to the Guinness Book of Records, because if they have a category for worst single day possible in a human being's life, I am SO totally the winner!

Sam stopped typing. She pulled a brown paper bag out from under her bed and carefully wrapped it around the bottle of orange cream soda she'd sneaked into her room. As she took a slurp, she looked around. After spending the entire evening covering the walls with enough horse posters and book jackets to hide almost all of the pink, the room wasn't as unliveable as it had seemed this morning.

Sam put the lid back on her bottle, gingerly slid it back under her bed, and returned to her typing.

So, here I am, sitting at my new desk, in my new room, in my new house! Hard to believe a single day can be both unbelievably exciting and totally

She froze while she thought about a better word for "totally" than "totally." "Aha!" she cried as she found her perfect word, hit the delete key seven times, and resumed blogging.

utterly horrific. It's too much for any person, especially a person under the age of eighteen, to have to comprehend.

I've decided to leave up all my old blogs because

if this freaky experience melts my brain, I want some proof that, at one point in my life, I was a clear-thinking, normal person. After what I've been through today, I'm pretty sure that I've been permanently scarred.

Mom has yet to apologize for this mess. I mean, I know she feels bad about how upset I am with this whole "living in a TV show," but she isn't taking any responsibility for it. She swears that she believed the deal she signed was for the camera crew to follow Danni around and that Robert tricked her into signing papers that included the rest of the family. I can believe that, but it doesn't mean I have to like it. If Robert really did trick Mom, why doesn't she fire him? Did she really read the papers before she signed them? I was going to ask her all this, but I chickened out. Yes, I admit it, I didn't have the guts. Come on, it's been a pretty tough day and I was afraid if I asked Mom anything, she'd get all emotional and start crying, and then I'd start crying, and…you know…it'd be a big tear fest.

Mom did say we'd have a family meeting sometime soon to discuss everything once we'd settled in and I'd calmed down. Well, I'm calm, but I'm still super-unhappy with the situation.

Sam looked up from the laptop and yelled out to Blu, "I'm not sure if you can read what I'm writing, so I'll sum it up for you. I'm very unhappy about being on TV!"

Blu's disembodied voice filled the room. "Please don't yell at me. There are microphones everywhere. Believe me, I can hear you. Besides, you really shouldn't be talking to me. You're not supposed to know I'm here."

Sam spun her chair around so that she faced the mirror. She stared straight into it and stuck her tongue out.

Blu laughed. "Just so you know, that's really not attractive."

Sam giggled. She got up from her chair and sat on the sill of her big, beautiful window. The sound of laughter pulled her gaze down to the swimming pool where she saw Rose and Danni playfully dunking their

feet and having a relaxed, silly moment.

Sam didn't mean to speak out loud, but the sight of her mom and sister having fun together was something she'd waited so long for, that she found herself surprisingly emotional.

"They seem happy enough," she said in a soft voice.

Blu's voice was equally muted. "Who?"

Sam answered while continuing to stare out her window. "Mom and Danni. I don't know if it's being back together, or this great new house, but it's so nice to see them smiling again. The past couple of weeks every single phone call between the two of them ended with a fight. I hate conflict in general, but Mom and Danni have always gotten along so super-great that all the tension has been thoroughly upsetting to me." Sam leaned back and looked up. "What a great night. I can't remember a clearer sky with so many stars." The sound of a horse's whinny brought her gaze back down to Earth. She grinned as she squinted to see the outline of the few horses that were out grazing in pasture. "I am seriously starting to like this house."

There was a long pause before Blu spoke. "Listen," he said hesitantly, "I do sincerely understand that today has been a nightmare for you, and, after our one-week agreement, if you tell me you don't want to do the show, I will keep my word and leave, but I think there's something more you should know."

Sam kept her focus outside on the horses happily munching on the sweet grass. "Hmm?"

Blu seemed to have trouble finding his words. "It's...the fact is...if you don't do the show, you'll have to move."

Sam sat up and stared into the mirror. "What?!"

"The T2CT Network owns this house, Sam, not your mom, not your sister. You all are living here for free in exchange for your participation in the show. If there's no show, then there's no house."

"You'd do that to us?" Sam spat in anger.

Blu spoke gently, "Don't get mad at me. I don't own this place, I just work here."

Sam looked out the window again. Her eyes wandered back and forth, from Rose and Danni at the pool to the SuAn Stables sign. She put her head in her hands and sighed. She spoke without looking up.

"So, I say 'no' to the show and we have to move... no great house, no big yard, no watching horses out of

my bedroom window. I say 'yes' and I have TV cameras in my face and pink carpet. That sound about right?"

Blu let out a sigh. "Yeah, that's pretty much everything."

There was a very long pause.

Sam nodded and looked back out the window. As she watched Rose and Danni dunking their feet, she realized that, for the first time in her entire life, she had the power to make a major decision that would make them truly happy.

"Man," she spoke toward the mirror, "it's not every day a twelve-year-old has the fate of her family in her hands." She thought for a moment before continuing. "This is entirely too much pressure for me to deal with."

Sam hopped down from the window sill. She paced back and forth several times. Blu watched her with more than a little worry. The kid, er…pre-teenager, seemed like she was getting more upset by the moment. Blu mentally kicked himself for telling her the truth about the house, even though he knew that it was the right thing to have done.

"Sam?" he asked, hoping she'd snap out of her agitated state.

Sam acted as if she hadn't heard him. She kept pacing and seemed to be speaking to herself. "I swore to Mom I'd never do this again, but I can't help it. I'm stressed out and need to relax."

There was a hint of alarm in Blu's voice. "What do you mean? What are you going to do?"

"None of your beeswax," Sam said as she walked toward the door.

Blu's voice sounded even more worried. "Sam! Come on, seriously, where are you going? What are you going to do? You aren't going to do something stupid, are you?"

"Umm…" Sam mulled over her thoughts for a moment. "Well, it may not be the smartest thing to do, but I'm twelve and this is what I do when life gets to be too much for me."

She headed out of the room, but a huge commotion behind the mirror caused her to turn back. She was surprised to see Blu lifting the mirror and peeking out into her room. He had cable, wires, and cords all wrapped around him, one pulling on his neck pretty hard. He called out before seeing that she was right next to him.

"Sam! Oh. Hi." He tried unsuccessfully to act as though nothing was bothering him. "Just out of curiosity, what exactly are you going to do to de-stress your young self?"

Sam crossed her arms, tilted her chin down, and looked up at Blu with bored annoyance. "As I said, Mr. Bluford, I do believe that what I do is none of your business."

She turned to leave. Blu hollered, "Wait!" as he reached out to grab her shoulder. He missed and fell flat on his face. Sam heard the loud thud and spun around to find Blu lying face down on the ugly pink carpet, rubbing his nose to make sure it wasn't broken. Sam hurriedly moved toward him.

"What happened?" she asked.

Blu, still rubbing his nose, replied, "For a such a gifted pre-teenager, that's a rather boneheaded question, don't you think?"

Sam put her hands over her mouth in an unsuccessful attempt to hide her giggles. Blu sat up and slid back onto the floor of the control room as Sam's chuckles grew in volume and intensity. By the time Blu finally got the feeling back in his nose,

Sam was wiping laughter tears off her cheeks.

"As it appears I haven't done any permanent damage to my poor snout, will you please tell me what it is you are going to do?" Blu implored.

Sam couldn't understand why he was so interested. "What's the big deal?"

Blu let out an aggravated groan. "I'm worried about you, okay? I know you're upset and I want to make sure you're not going to do anything to hurt yourself."

"Me? Really? You're worried about *me*?" Sam was both surprised and pleased to think that she might have found a true friend in the ultra-cool Malcolm Bluford.

"Yes, goofball. I don't want to spend the rest of my life feeling guilty because a fiendishly smart ki—" Blu caught himself, "pre-teenager did something really dumb and messed up her life because of me."

Sam was smiling her biggest grin of the whole day. She enjoyed knowing that Blu liked her. "Just how messed up will my life be for sneaking downstairs and snagging a pint of chocolate-chip cookie-dough ice cream?"

It was Blu's turn to be surprised. "Ice cream? That's

the terrible thing you swore to your mother you'd never do again? *Eat ice cream?*"

"Hey," Sam shot back defensively, "we're talking about a *whole pint* of ice cream! I can do it! I can eat an entire container. Of course, it gives me a nasty stomachache and massively stinky farts for two days, but I can do it!"

Blu took a moment to look over the situation. There he was, the top director of reality television, sitting on the floor of his control room, dealing with a twelve-year-old who was threatening him with forty-eight hours of farts. He smirked and shook his head. "For someone who prides herself on being so witty, I'd think you'd at least use a better word than fart," he teased Sam.

"Such as…?" she responded, enjoying the friendly attention.

Blu lifted his eyebrows and looked across at Sam with his best academic, professorial face. "My personal favorite is the scientific term for this particular body function: 'gastric disturbance'."

Sam nodded as she repeated the new term. "'Gastric disturbance'. I like it! Sounds very medical and serious."

She turned to leave, but stopped.

"Umm…Blu? I happen to know that there are two pints of chocolate-chip cookie-dough in the freezer. Want me to snag one for you?"

Blu smiled his biggest grin of the day. "No, thanks, but I appreciate the offer. It's time for me to go. I'll see you in the morning."

Sam gave a little wave and left the room.

As she sneaked down the stairs to the kitchen, a simple thought about Blu floated through her mind: *Who would have ever thought we could be friends?* Little did she know, at that very moment, Blu was thinking the very same thing.

CHAPTER 10

Click click click, clack clack click.

This is day #2 of my agreement with Blu and it's
not starting out too good.

Sam froze. She thought for a moment; there had to
be a more interesting word for "good" than "good"; but
she couldn't think of anything. She double-clicked on
her mouse so that the word "good" was highlighted,
and then clicked on the "thesaurus" button on her
word processor. Several options came up, but none of
them seemed quite right. She tapped her forehead with

her finger. "Think!" she said to herself. Suddenly, an awesome word popped into her head. She deleted "it's not starting out too good" and resumed typing.

it's not an auspicious beginning. Mom just yelled up to Danni and me that breakfast this morning is going to be an official family meeting. Instead of coming out of her room to answer, Danni buzzed Mom on the intercom (yes, this house is so big it has an intercom system so you can talk to people without having to get off your lazy rear end). Danni whined that she couldn't come downstairs for a family meeting until she was properly dressed, and that included hair and makeup. Do you believe it? Because of the cameras in the house, my sister won't even come down to breakfast without getting all done up! How lame is that? Now, our breakfast is scheduled (*scheduled!*) for 8:30 a.m., and it's only 8:16 a.m. That means I am going to starve for the next fourteen minutes! There is no way I'm going to survive another four days of this.

I'm guessing this family meeting will be about the whole reality TV show nightmare. What am I going to say? How does a person tell her mom that she's made the biggest mistake in the whole world, without hurting her feelings?

From deep inside Sam's stomach rumbled up a gigantic gurgle that was so loud, Blu heard it from inside the control room. Sam grimaced as the mirror slid out and up and Blu's booming laughter filled her room.

"Here." He tossed her a banana while laughing. "You need this a heck of a lot more than I do."

For less than a millisecond, Sam considered acting annoyed at his blatant laughing at her, but she was so seriously hungry that she ditched the thought and leaped at the banana as it flew through the air. She caught it just before her body fell in a heap onto her bed. Blu stood in the doorway of the control room laughing harder and applauding.

"Brilliant!" Blu proclaimed in his best sports-announcer voice. "Sam's dazzling display of athletic ability has brought the crowd to its feet!" Blu raised his arms to do the wave while cheering madly.

Sam smiled as she wolfed down the banana. "You look so normal. Who'd guess that underneath that cool dude outside, beats the heart of a total goofus?"

Blu gasped and grabbed his chest, as if to protect his sensitive soul from the horrific accusation hurled at him. He tried to appear as if Sam's words had caused him great emotional as well as physical pain, but he couldn't do it for more than a second; he began to laugh again and had to admit, "I really am a giant dweeb, aren't I?"

Sam opened her mouth to answer, when an incredibly loud series of honks from a car horn startled her. She looked up at Blu. "Who would be so rude as to sit in front of our house, honking away, before breakfast?"

The deadpan, "Duh" expression that flashed across Blu's face surprised Sam for a moment, until she realized she already knew the answer to her question.

"No!" Sam jumped up and began angrily pacing around her room. "Nobody should have to deal with Robert first thing in the morning. That's the kind of thing that can ruin a person's whole day. Who invited him, anyway?" The more Sam thought about Robert, the more agitated she became. Along with increasing the speed of her pacing, she began to flail her arms and the intensity of her voice rose from loud to pretty-darn-close-to-yelling. "This is a family meeting," she continued, "and the last time I checked, Rotten Robert Ruebens was not a member of my family! He better not try to have a say in anything we discuss, and he seriously better not try to vote on anything in this meeting, or I'll have a major cow! I need a plan to deal with this! Yes, a plan, but I don't have time to make a plan! Think! *Think!* Urgh!"

"Hey!" Blu shouted to get Sam's attention. It worked; Sam was jolted back into the reality of the moment. Blu pointed at Sam. "You are not going to have a cow. You are going to close your eyes, take slow, deep breaths, and pull yourself together."

Blu opened his arms wide and drew in a huge, slow breath. Sam watched him, then closed her eyes and mimicked his actions as best she could. The two of them stood there, doing these long, slow breaths for a full minute.

"There." Blu opened his eyes and looked at Sam with a calm serenity. "Feel better?"

Sam opened her eyes and stared intently into Blu's. "I'm not sure how I feel," she said with extreme gravity, "because I'm so dizzy I think I'm going to barf up banana." She giggled as she stuck out her tongue, and lowered her arms to hold her stomach.

Blu chortled. "I'd rather see you dizzy than angry, so, hurl away if you have to!" His tone softened as he looked at his watch. "Uh, Sam? It's time for your meeting."

Sam stopped giggling. She took one last super-gargantuan, calming breath, turned and walked out of her room. *This is so silly*, she thought to herself as she slid down the banister to the ground floor, *we've had a million family meetings. There is no need for this one to be any different from the others. I'm taking this situation way too seriously. It'll be me and Mom and Danni talking, laughing, and dealing with whatever problems we have, just as it's always been.*

Sam's internal pep talk lifted her spirits. She jumped off the banister and bounced past the formal dining room on her way to the kitchen.

"Samantha," Rose called out.

"Coming, Mom," Sam yelled back.

"But you just passed us," Rose replied.

Sam stopped. She looked back and forth. The house was big, but was it that big that she'd gotten lost? "But Mom," she bellowed, "isn't the kitchen in the back of the house?"

From behind her came Robert's blustering, "Hey, Columbus, while you're discovering the route to the kitchen, the rest of us are waiting for you in the dining room."

The sound of that voice zapped all the positive thoughts right out of Sam's brain. She bit her lower lip to stop herself from yelling something equally snotty; she knew that would upset Rose and then the whole day would be ruined. Those few steps back down the hallway to the dining room suddenly seemed to be a very long and spooky path that led to certain doom. Sam glanced up to see a large mirror hanging on the wall in front of her. She studied its frame for a moment before seeing what she was looking for, one of Blu's hidden TV cameras. She stared directly into the camera and whispered just loud enough for the hidden microphone to hear. "Blu, I got my plan: I do a couple more super-fast deep breaths, get dizzy, and barf all over you-know-who."

Robert's great big head peered out from the dining room. "I'm sure you're enjoying your conversation with yourself, but we're starving, so hustle in here, please."

Sam turned back toward the dining room, thinking how only Robert could use the word *please* in a way that didn't sound the slightest bit polite. "Mom," she said as she walked into the room, "why are we eating breakfast in the dining..." But Sam was so stunned by what she saw as she stepped into the room that she not only forgot what she was saying, she also forgot to put her left foot out in front of her right. In other words, Sam fell flat on her face.

In the middle of her oh-so-ungraceful voyage to the ground, Sam heard her mother let out a horrified shriek. The sound resonated in Sam's heart; even though she was unhappy with her mom, she certainly didn't want to do anything to hurt or frighten her. It was this desire to spare Rose any pain or worry that gave Sam the strength to bounce up from the ground as quickly as a bunny – and you know how fast those bunnies can move. And, while the smashing of her chin against the hard wooden floor had really hurt, Sam

made a big show of laughing as if this had been the funniest thing she'd ever done.

Rose jumped up from her seat at the head of the outrageously long table. She tried to rush over to Sam, but her trademark high heels made any quick movement impossible. She held out her arms. "Samantha! You okay? Tell me you didn't hurt yourself!"

Rubbing her sore chin while trying to act cool and in control, Sam replied, "I'm fine, Mom. I was just goofing around."

Robert, leaning back in his chair next to Rose, chimed in sarcastically, "Thanks for the pre-breakfast floor show, Kiddo." He motioned to the chair opposite him down at the end of the table. "Now, if you don't mind, we have a great deal to discuss this morning."

Sam stood her ground for a moment to survey the scene that had caught her so off guard when she had first entered the room. Way down at the end of the table were Rose, Robert, and Danni. In front of them, the table was set for a formal meal with a whole bunch of different plates, forks, and glasses. Next to them, Michi and Lou were hovering around, videotaping everything. And what was it that had freaked out Sam

so much? Giant lights! All around Rose, Robert, and Danni were monstrous, free-standing movie lights. Sam had been expecting a quiet family breakfast but instead found herself in the middle of a full-blown movie shoot! Sam stared at her mother. How could Rose have allowed this? Family meetings had always been just for the family! Sam was now feeling completely, utterly, and one-hundred-and-ten-percently let down by her mom.

"Sam!" Danni barked from her seat. "Quit joking around! I'm hungry! Mom won't let anybody touch a thing until you take your seat."

"And my espresso isn't getting any warmer," added Robert.

Knowing that every second she was able to waste would cause Robert's espresso to get colder, Sam shuffled in super-slow motion to her seat. As she slid into her chair, the incredibly bright lights temporarily blinded her. She reached out to cover her eyes, but accidentally knocked over a large crystal goblet of water. The glass didn't break, but the water splattered across the table; unfortunately, a few drops flew far enough to reach the fancy, expensive tie hanging

around the neck of the person on that side of the table. Sam gasped and slapped her hands over her mouth to stop herself from giggling, but the noise was enough to get Robert's attention. He noticed that her eyes were focused on him. He looked down and saw the droplets soaking into the hand-woven silk.

Robert's head snapped back up; he glared at Sam with such a menacing expression that she was almost scared of him for a moment. Rose missed the spilling of the water, but she saw the look between Sam and Robert and recognized that if she didn't intervene, the meeting would dissolve into a terrible scene, maybe even something as awful as what had happened yesterday in front of the house. Rose couldn't handle anymore drama like that. She quickly raised her crystal goblet of orange juice and loudly declared, "I proclaim this Devine family meeting to order."

Everyone stared at Rose. She glanced around and motioned for them to pick up their own glasses of juice and join in her kick-off toast. Danni rolled her eyes in disbelief as she lifted her goblet. Robert got in a quick sneer at Sam before smiling the great white smile and raising his. Sam sighed in annoyance; *a million family*

meetings, she thought to herself, *a million family meetings and never once has Mom begun one like it was a ceremony*. Sam kept her elbow on the table, lifting her glass just the tiniest bit to make it appear as if she were participating.

Once she saw the glasses in the air, Rose repeated her proclamation in an even bigger, bolder, and shriller voice. "*Now*, I officially call this Devine family meeting to order." Rose opened a leather binder and appeared to flip through several papers; she grabbed one sheet and held it out in front of her. "The agenda for this extraordinary meeting," she continued as she scanned the paper in her hands, "is as follows. First, we will discuss our new living situation and our lovely new abode. Then we will talk about business, because Danni's career has become our family business. How does that sound to everyone?"

Sam's jaw dropped. Why was Rose making such a big deal out of a little family meeting? Sam turned to Danni to see if she was as confused by this strange behavior as she was, but Danni wasn't paying the slightest bit of attention. She was holding up a giant spoon and admiring her lipstick. Sam noticed how much makeup her sister was wearing. Danni's hair was curled, rouge sparkled on her cheeks, and she even had false eyelashes on! Sam's mind was spiraling; was this how life was going to be in this reality TV world? Even something as unglamorous as a dumb family breakfast meeting was going to be a major production? Wasn't the point of a reality show to allow people to see the reality of their lives?

"Mom," Sam spoke out, not even realizing she'd interrupted her mother, "what is this?"

Rose smiled lovingly at Sam. "What is what, Sammy?"

Sammy? Nobody ever called Sam "Sammy," not even when she'd been a baby. "What is all this? These lights, these fancy dishes, Danni's makeup, and your fancy dress. Why are you wearing high heels to eat cornflakes?"

Rose glanced uncomfortably at the video camera pointed at her. "Samantha darling, I don't know what you are talking about. This is just another typical day in our wonderful lives now that we have this fabulous new house to live in and your sister is a world-famous superstar."

Sam wasn't ready to give up. "We've never gotten

dressed up for breakfast. And you've never once 'officially proclaimed' anything. Why are we doing all this fake stuff?"

Rose tried to giggle away the unpleasant moment, but it only made her more aware of the camera directed at her. She closed her eyes, put the back of her hand to her forehead, and spoke to herself in a soft whisper. "I am calm and in control. I am calm and in control."

Robert kicked Sam from under the table to get her attention.

She growled back, "And why are *you* here? This is a family meeting. You don't belong here."

Robert opened his mouth, but Rose kicked him under the table. Robert closed his mouth and forced a thin, pained smirk.

Rose nodded. "That is true, Sam. Technically, Robert is not a member of this family. But since he is the key to making sure things go smoothly with Danni's career, it's important that he be at these meetings so we can all work together and everything in our lives can run according to plan."

"But whose plan, Mom? Who made this plan? I thought once Danni returned home we'd get to be a

normal family again. Eating breakfast in a dining room that's as big as a restaurant, that's not normal. Getting all dressed up at eight o'clock in the morning, that's not normal. What happened to the *normal* part of the plan?"

"Honey," Rose cooed, "I understand that this new life is going to require a little getting used to. You've spent your whole life living in little apartments where we didn't have such nice things. But now that we have them, shouldn't we enjoy them?"

Danni glared at her sister. "Listen up, Little Bit, if you don't want to look your best or live the good life, at least don't spoil it for the rest of us!"

That statement made Sam feel horrible; she didn't want to spoil life for her mom or her sister. She hung her head sadly and didn't say another word.

Rose's focus went back to her list. "First topic, our new living situation." She smiled as she put down the paper. "I think we've already begun that discussion. Do you girls like your rooms?"

Danni began to bubble with enthusiasm. "My room is awesome! I have the biggest mirror and the best lighting! My closet is bigger than our old apartment! And having Jean and Jehan right next door to help with my hair and makeup is the best! You did great getting us this house!"

Rose beamed. Sam was pleasantly surprised to see her sister acting like her old self again, silly, funny, and respectful to their mom. Rose faced Sam and waited for her response. Sam recognized that this was it; this was her moment to dig into her mom and find out why she'd agreed to this insane reality TV! Sure, Rose had managed to make certain that Sam got the room that overlooked the stables, but still, it was pink and Rose knew how much Sam hated pink! Sam could lay it all out and tell her mother how unhappy she was, and demand that they end the stupid TV show! Yes, this was the moment!

But as Sam began to speak, she looked at her mom and saw a deep desire for something positive. Rose desperately wanted Sam to tell her that everything was wonderful. Sam rubbed her eyes to buy herself a moment to think. If Rose really needed to hear she'd made her daughter happy, how could Sam not give her that? Even though she was miserable, even though she wanted to scream about the unfairness of having video cameras in her face, Sam couldn't do it. All those times when Rose had worked so hard to earn money to feed the family, all of that was behind them now and the only thing her mother wanted was to know that Sam was content.

"Yeah, Mom," she said softly, "my room rocks. Thank you very much."

Rose was so thrilled that for the first time in a long time, both of her daughters were home and happy, she became teary. She beamed and waved her hands in front of her face to dry her eyes before her mascara began to run.

An awkward silence fell over the room. Robert, sensing the opportunity to seize control of the situation, grabbed a basket.

"Muffins, anyone?" he asked with that big white grin back on his face. He handed the basket to Rose and continued talking. "I assume it's safe to move on to agenda item number two. I have exciting news to share. We have an amazing opportunity regarding Danni's career." Robert slipped out of his seat, walked over to a side table. When he returned to the dining-room table, he was carrying a colossal platter with a big silver cover.

Robert set this in front of Danni. He lifted the cover and said, "Behold!"

On the platter was a bottle of maple syrup.

Danni bit her upper lip as she examined the bottle. "This means what? I'm going to eat pancakes? How does that help my career, Robert?"

Robert laughed his hearty, fake laugh. "Danni, you are so wry." He pretended to wipe tears from his eyes. "No, my dear; look at the bottle."

Danni picked up the bottle and held it to the light. She shook it, opened it, sniffed the contents, put the cap back on, and set it on the table. She nodded several times as if she were beginning to understand.

"Nope," she shook her head, "no idea. What is this?"

Robert grandly gestured to the bottle. "This is the finest maple syrup on the planet!"

Rose, Danni, and Sam continued to sit silently.

He stood back smugly, waiting for someone to figure out what this represented. Aggravated that no one understood, he tapped his foot. "Think about it. Maple syrup. The finest maple syrup in the whole world."

More confused silence.

Finally, in exasperation, he shouted, "Canada! Great maple syrup comes from Canada, people! See the maple leaf on the bottle? That tells you it comes from Canada! You, Danni, are going to perform tomorrow night in Canada's largest city, Toronto, at the Skydome, one of the world's most beautiful arenas, for an audience of some thirty thousand people!"

Rose jumped up and applauded. "Robert! That's fabulous! Thirty thousand people! Why, that's better than a chocolate-covered cherry atop a super-sized sundae!"

"Thirty thousand people?" cried Danni. "That's so cool! That's so amazing! That's...that's," the enormity of the situation hit Danni like a ton of bricks, "that's so impossible! I can't be ready tomorrow night! We just sent the band and the dancers home! I can't do this alone!" Danni began to wail, "How could you do this to me, Robert? How could you set me up to fail like this?"

Rose hustled over to comfort Danni. Robert was truly stunned. He had not expected any kind of negative reaction.

"But Danni, you're a star, a superstar! Everyone loves

you! What's there to be worried about?"

Danni looked up at Robert, but her perfectly made-up face was now a mess of tears and runny colors. One of her fake eyelashes was hanging off her chin. "Are you kidding me? I've never performed in an arena! The biggest show I've ever done was at the stadium here in town, the other night, for a measly ten thousand people! It's one thing to make a couple of music videos and then spend the next year perfecting my performance, night after night, with the same band and the same dancers, it's an entirely different thing to go out onstage alone in front of thirty thousand people! I've sacrificed so much to become a star and I'm going to lose it all with one horrific performance! I'll be the laughing stock of the entire planet!" Danni stopped wailing to blow her nose into her napkin, but then continued. "And you said this was in Canada? Well, that's even worse! I'm going to look like a complete idiot when I try to say something and everyone realizes that I don't know how to *speak* Canadian!"

Without meaning to, Sam laughed out loud. Robert, Rose, and Danni glared at her.

"I'm sorry! I'm so sorry! I'm so, so sorry!" Sam

apologized with all her might. "That was an accident. I didn't mean to laugh. I'm not laughing at you, Danni. It's…that, um…Danni? There is no such thing as *speaking* Canadian."

"There isn't?" Danni sniffled.

"Nope." Sam shook her head. "The two languages of Canada are English and French, and most people know both."

"Oh." Danni stopped crying. She thought about what had just taken place and began to giggle. "So I guess there won't be too much of a language barrier."

Everyone in the room, even Michi and Lou, let out a sigh of relief. Robert sat back down in his chair, acting all cool and in control, but Sam noticed that as he reached for his espresso, his hand was shaking. *He's nervous,* she thought to herself, *he's really anxious about something. There's more going on here than he's letting on.*

"So, Robert," Sam asked, trying to sound completely innocent, "how did a concert for thirty thousand people suddenly spring up out of nowhere?"

Robert's posture stiffened. He wasn't sure what the kid was doing, but he knew that if he didn't handle

this well, Danni would start crying again and he'd be in real trouble.

"These things happen in show business. When an opportunity presents itself you have to rise to the occasion. That's what it takes to become and then stay a superstar."

Sam glanced over at her mom and sister. She knew they were listening intently. Danni looked confused. Rose had concern written all over her face. Sam could see that both of them wanted everything to be all right; it didn't matter how things were worked out, everything needed to be okay. But still, something strange was going on with Robert. Maybe, if for once she could get the truth out of him, maybe things would work out for everyone.

"Yeah," she said slowly, "but thirty thousand tickets. That's a lot of seats to fill on such short notice. How are you going to get that many people to come to a concert that's only been set up the day before?"

Rose and Danni simultaneously turned to Robert. He swallowed hard. Sam could see he was searching his brain for the right thing to say.

He flashed that winning smile again. "Don't you

worry about those pesky details. I'm in complete control and can guarantee every seat in the place will be filled."

Rose raised an eyebrow and crossed her arms in front of her body. "It seems the last time I trusted you with *those pesky details*, I ended up sharing half of my home with a camera crew. Perhaps you should share the burden a bit, Robert."

Robert carefully set down his cup. Sam could almost smell the smoke pouring out of his ears as his brain worked hard to come up with an explanation.

He tried to chuckle, but the noise sounded more like gagging than laughing. He knew he'd been cornered. "Fine. I have nothing to hide. What do you need to know? Let's see…well, this isn't exactly a full-blown concert, but it's still a very big deal."

He shot a quick, snotty glance at Sam and then turned his full attention and complete charm on Rose and Danni. "It's the half-time show of the Canadian Football League's Toronto Argonauts. Our talented Miss Devine," Robert smiled directly at Danni, "*her band* and *her dancers* only have to do a couple of numbers. It's a major career milestone and it will be televised throughout the United States and Canada."

Danni's outlook immediately improved. "A half-time show? With my band? That sounds like a lot less pressure! Why didn't you say so?"

Robert made a lame attempt to appear humble. "Because, Danni, with everything that's happened and you finally getting to move into your new home, I was afraid that you wouldn't think it was a big enough gig for you to be willing to pack up and travel again right away. And I knew that this was a once-in-a-lifetime opportunity that I couldn't let you pass up. Forgive me?"

Danni gave Robert one of her sweetest smiles. "Really? You were thinking of *me*? Oh Robert, you are just too much."

Sam crossed her eyes and stuck out her tongue, but no one noticed.

Rose was still wary. "Hang on, Robert. Why didn't you mention this to *me* before now?"

Sam put her elbows on the table and leaned forward. This was going to be it; this was the moment where Rose was finally going to see Robert for his true, creepy self.

"Because, Rose," Robert began slowly, "I thought it

would be best to wait with the information until—" Robert began to cough. He grabbed his goblet and drank down the water as if his life depended upon it. He set down the glass, cleared his throat, straightened his tie, and smiled at Rose.

Still standing beside Danni, Rose remained stoic; she didn't move a muscle as she waited for Robert to complete his explanation. Sam was enjoying the moment beyond all measure.

Robert recognized he was still on the hook and continued, slowly. "As I was saying, I didn't think it was wise to tell you about the opportunity because I wanted to be responsible and I—"

"Sorry to interrupt, Robert," Danni chimed in as she reached for a slice of toast, "but I'm insanely hungry." She turned to her sister, "Sam, please pass the jelly."

Robert's eyes suddenly lit up. "Passports! Yes! Passports! Because everyone knows you can't travel to another country without a passport and Canada is another country so you need a passport!" Robert's entire demeanor improved as he realized he had concocted a solid excuse. "That is what occurred!

I wasn't sure if I could get passports for you and Danni and, of course, dear little Sammy here, so I waited before mentioning anything. I would never want to get everyone's hopes up for something as exciting as this, and then not deliver!"

Sam could tell this was a complete load of hooey. Robert was *totally lying*! It was so obvious! She excitedly waited for her mother to rip into him for being such a big rotten fibber.

"Robert Ruebens," Rose exclaimed. "Passports? You got us passports? That is so thrilling! Now we can travel anywhere in the world! Robert, forgive me for doubting you."

Sam was flabbergasted! Her mother believed this oh-so-obvious, pathetic lie? Sam sat perfectly still, watching in disbelief and horror as her mother, her sister, and Robert began mapping out all the scheduling details of the quick trip up to The Great White North. Robert had chartered a private jet so they could leave anytime tomorrow morning. Of course, Danni's hair and makeup artists, Jean and Jehan, would travel along.

Robert was enjoying telling everyone what he'd arranged. "After the show Saturday night, we can relax

at the hotel. Sunday, Danni will do a couple of press interviews, then we'll do a quick motor coach tour of the city, have a lovely dinner, and fly home late Sunday night."

Sam jumped up from her seat. "Whoops, sorry, can't go!"

After forgetting that she was even in the room, everyone was a bit spooked by Sam's sudden declaration. Rose was the first person to find her voice. "What?"

Sam shook her head to try to appear sorry about this turn of events. "Can't go. Sorry, but I promised a friend I'd be somewhere Sunday night. See, I have a friend who is in a show and I promised him I'd be there, to watch him perform, and you know that once a commitment is made, we aren't allowed to break it." Sam knew that calling Mr. Wannabee her *friend* was stretching the truth pretty darn close to the breaking point, but she *had* made a promise. Besides, she didn't want to go anywhere or do anything arranged by that creepy, lying Robert.

"We'll miss ya, kid. Be safe." Robert could barely hide his pleasure at not having Sam along.

 176

"Oh, no, young lady." Rose refused to entertain the thought of leaving Sam behind. "If we have to leave Canada early Sunday morning so you can keep your promise, then so be it. This family has already spent one year apart and that is more than enough. Subject closed."

Both Sam and Robert pouted for a moment, but neither one was willing to fight Rose on this issue. Sam felt more trapped within her life than ever. Things were not moving smoothly along her path to "being normal again."

"I'm going to the stables," she called out as she walked away from the table.

Rose, Danni, and Robert were so busy making decisions about the trip up to The Great White North that not one of them heard her. Sam sighed as she left the room.

She walked back over to the large mirror with the hidden camera and held up her watch so that it could be seen.

"Hey, Blu," she whispered loudly into the microphone, "can you see what time it is? It's only ten o'clock in the morning. That means that day number two of our agreement isn't even half over, and it's already twice as awful as day number one! Isn't that amazing?"

CHAPTER 11

Click click click, clack clack click.

It's the night of Day #2, a day that started out so horribly I can't even begin to explain, BUT something hilarious happened this afternoon that almost makes all the bad stuff worthwhile.

After I left that pathetic excuse of a family meeting this morning, I went into the kitchen to snag an apple before going over to the stables to go riding with Olga. See, with all the chaos of our meeting, I never got to eat and I really was hungry!

Anyway, in the kitchen I see a package with my name on it, so I open it. It was full of new riding clothes, real riding clothes. For the first time ever, I looked like one of those girls I see in the magazines (I get all the horse-riding mags I can find). Mom must have ordered this stuff for me from some catalog. This is one of the things that makes suddenly having money kind of fun, but I hope I never get so spoiled that getting new stuff stops being fun and just becomes another everyday thing. That would be sad.

I go to the SuAn Stables and pick out my horse for the day (I got Thunder Bay! Love him!) and as I'm warming him up in the ring, Robert and Mom pull up in Robert's newest fancy, itty-bitty, "I'm too cool for a back seat" car. I know this can't be good... Robert would never be caught dead in a place like the stables where a speck of dust could land on one of his custom-made suits. So I put a smile on my face, ride Thunder Bay over, and say hello.

Mom was all red and babbling. I couldn't understand a thing she was saying. Robert puts his slimy hand on her shoulder to calm her down and tells me that Danni's first CD has just gone platinum. Now, I don't live under a rock, so I do know that this is a good thing (it means the CD has sold a million copies), but apparently I didn't understand just how **truly** great this is because I said, "That's cool!" and Mom looked crushed (I guess she expected a bigger reaction) and Robert looked even MORE disdainful than usual. Seeing that I'd somehow managed to disappoint my mom (as if I care what Robert thinks), I tried to salvage the moment by throwing my arms in the air and yelling, "I mean that is TOTALLY WAY COOL," at the top of my lungs. Guess what? That frightened poor old Thunder Bay so much that he reared up. Yeah, he was totally standing straight in the air with his front hooves kicking at the clouds.

I didn't have time to react and got thrown to the ground. Luckily, I landed in something soft so I

didn't get hurt. UNluckily, the soft thing that broke my fall was a huge pile of horse poop. Yup, me...brand-new riding outfit...straight into the biggest pile of horse poop you've ever seen (sigh). And I've since found out these fancy new riding clothes don't wash very well. Basically — they are completely ruined.

But wait — remember I said there was a good part to the day? Guess who had to drive me home — in his new car?!? LOL! I was tightly wrapped in a horse blanket to ensure that none of the evil horse droppings came close to touching any of the fine leather in his car, but Robert couldn't deal with the smell. The whole way home he was grumbling about having to play chauffeur. That alone made the whole mess worth living through. And don't worry — Thunder Bay was fine. I gave him a couple of carrots and told him I was really sorry. I swear, the look in that horse's eye told me he understood. If only more people were as smart and understanding as horses, life would be so much easier.

Sam sneaked a slurp of soda from the bottle that was still hiding under her bed. She giggled as she read her blog one last time before posting it.

"Hey, Blu," she called out toward the giant bedroom mirror, "you have to read my blog tonight. It's really funny."

Blu's friendly voiced filled the room. "Did you report your great tumble into the pile of horse droppings?"

Sam's jaw dropped. "How did you know about that?"

The mirror slid out and up. From inside the control room, Blu yelled for Sam to join him inside his brain.

Sam hopped inside. "Tell me," she whined, "how did you know about my fall?"

Blu reached over and hit the "play" button on one of the many videotape machines stacked against the wall. "There," he said as he pointed to the video monitor on the other side of the room.

Sam watched the twenty-second snippet of video that showed her tumbling off Thunder Bay and landing in the soft poop. "All right, smart guy," she asked, "how did you get this? There was no camera crew following me around at the stables."

Blu leaned back in his chair. "True, but I think you're forgetting how close the stables are to this house and how powerful the zoom is on some of my cameras."

Blu turned his chair and pointed to one of the monitors. It showed a wide shot of the backyard. He reached out with his left hand and pushed a small lever. The scene on the monitor changed. Instead of looking at her backyard, Sam was now looking at a super-zoomed-in view of the main ring over at the stables.

"That's not fair." Sam pouted. "I know you have cameras around the pool, but to tape me anywhere, even over the fence at the stables? I don't think that's fair at all."

She turned to march out of the control room, feeling betrayed.

"Yo," Blu called to her, "before you go away thinking I'm picking on you, how would you like to see some other video I took outside using one of my super-zoom cameras?"

Sam shrugged. She didn't want Blu to see how badly he'd hurt her feelings. She felt foolish for thinking she could trust him when it was obvious that he was only

being nice to her so she'd stick around for his stupid TV show. "Sure. Whatever."

Flashing an "I'm so proud of myself" grin, Blu swiveled around in his chair and hit the "play" button on a different video recorder. "Ta dah!" he sang out as he raised his arms to get Sam to look at one of the other monitors in the room.

Sam had no idea what he could possibly be so excited to show her. However, Blu's impression of one of those game-show ladies who prance around *oohing* and *ahhing* as they point to the fabulous prizes was enough to make Sam look at the screen. It took a moment for her to recognize what was in front of her; it was tape of Robert walking in the backyard.

"Blu!" she spluttered. "Dealing with him in person isn't bad enough? You're going to make me watch Robert on TV?"

"Chill, my young friend," intoned Blu. "Watch. Listen. Learn."

Sam cocked her head to the side and let out a wet, sloppy raspberry, but she did return her focus to the TV. Robert was walking away from the house, far away from the house. He kept turning his head from side to

side, as if he wanted to be sure that no one was following him. He quickly hopped behind a large bush, but the camera zoomed in enough so that he could still be seen.

"What's he doing?" she asked as she stepped a little closer to the monitor. Sam saw Robert lift his wrist-phone to his mouth. "What is he doing?" She repeated her question with a little more annoyance behind it. "Why is he hiding behind a bush to make a phone call?"

"Maybe if you'd stop using your mouth and start using your ears, you'd find out," Blu retorted plainly.

Sam nodded, never taking her eyes off Robert for a second. She leaned in even more to hear what he was going to say.

"Judy! Judy," Robert hissed into his wrist-phone. "Listen to me. We have an emergency situation. I need you to get passports for the Devine family immediately!"

Sam gasped. She snapped her head around to stare at Blu. "But he said he *already had* our passports! He said that he waited to tell us about Canada until he had them! That was *why* he waited to tell us!"

Blu put a finger up to his mouth to hush Sam. He used his other hand to point back at the monitor. An astounded Sam turned back to see what was coming next from the big liar.

Robert was nodding as if he were listening to the person on the other end of the wrist-phone conversation. "I know," he snarled, "I know it's difficult, but this is urgent." He paused again to listen. When he did answer, his voice was venomous. "Don't tell me it can't be done in less then twenty-four hours? I'm *Robert K. Ruebens*! You simply expain to the passport people that you work for Robert K. Ruebens! Nobody says, 'no' to me!" He listened again. His body language made it pretty darned obvious that he didn't like what he was hearing. "All right, all right!" he snapped. "I'll cover all the costs out of my own pocket – just get it done!"

"Now," he continued, a bit calmer, "get me these passports by tomorrow morning, or get yourself a new job!" Robert pushed a button on his wrist-phone to end the call, but he did it with such force he actually hurt himself. He sneaked back toward the house, shaking his wrist in pain.

Sam turned to Blu. She was so angry, it took a moment for her to find her voice. Blu quietly waited for her to put her whirling thoughts into words.

"I *knew* he was lying!" she spat out. "Knew it! Knew it! *Knew it!*" Sam stomped around the control room. "Such a creep! Such a total, unbelievable, undeniable *creep*! He's such a creep that he's a creep and a *half*!" Something major flashed across her brain. She stopped stomping and drilled her eyes into Blu. "You have to give me that tape. I have to show that to my mom. Yes, that's *it*! Once my mom sees the tape, then she'll know what a total creep Robert is, and fire him! Then, with him gone, Danni won't have to go off and do more concerts, and our TV show will end, and our lives will go back to normal! This is awesome!"

"Whoa, cowgirl." Blu cautiously stood up from his chair. "Slow down. You need to seriously chill before you do something you might regret."

A supremely stunned Sam stared at Blu incredulously. Had he completely lost his mind? Didn't he understand how badly she wanted this whole "famous" life to go away?

"Did you not see the same thing I did?" Sam

spluttered. "That creep lied to us! He deserves to be fired! How would you like somebody lying to you?"

"I'm not saying you don't have a right to be mad," Blu responded gently and deliberately, "but Sam, think about the consequences of your actions. If you tell your mom, and she gets mad and fires Robert, where does that leave your family? Danni loves her singing career; your mom is loving getting to buy fancy clothes and living in a big house. Are you prepared to destroy all that they've worked for just to get back at some smarmy dude? As bright as you are, I'd have thought you'd be able to figure out a better way to handle this situation."

Sam wasn't sure if Blu was trying to help her or manage her. After all, he did stand to lose his job if the family quit the TV show. Yet, he had been the only person to really listen to her lately and he had said he'd rather quit a job that made him miserable than stick it out for the money. She wanted to believe he was her friend. She desperately needed an ally, someone she knew was on her side.

"Okay, Blu," Sam said, pulling herself as straight and tall as she possibly could. "Let's say I am as bright

as I think I am. What would a super-brilliant me do in this situation?"

Blu grinned from ear to ear. "I believe the super-brilliant you already knows the answer to that question. Think about how well you handled me yesterday. What did you do when you realized that I wasn't going to leave the house just because you told me to?"

Sam tried to remember. "I…um…I…I cried?"

Blu almost chuckled, but he stopped himself. "Yeah, but that didn't work too well, so then what did you do?"

Sam tapped her forehead in her attempt to remember what she had done that had so impressed Blu. "Come on, brain," she said softly. "Think. What did I do? What did I *do*? What…oh!" Sam thrust both arms forward with her forefingers pointing directly at Blu. "I made a deal with you!"

Blu was nodding so hard Sam thought his head might just spring off. He seemed to be rather proud of her. Sam enjoyed the idea that she had done something that had impressed her cool friend, but she still didn't understand what he was attempting to tell her. She tried not to let it show.

"That's right. I made a deal with you. So, now," Sam spoke slowly in the hope that Blu would jump in and flat-out tell her what he was thinking, "now I…I make a deal with Robert…to try to get him, Robert, to…" Sam was annoyed that Blu wasn't jumping in. She stopped talking and stared blankly at him. He stared right back.

"Aurgh," she cried in frustration, "make a deal with Robert to *do what*? Help me!"

Blu sat back in his chair. "Make a deal with Robert to get something you need to make the whole situation less painful for you. If you get him fired, your mom and sister will be sad, so you don't want to go that far; but currently, you seem pretty darn unhappy. What could you get Robert to do that would make you less miserable?"

Sam bit her lip and looked down. What could she ask for, what would make her life better?

"Come on, Donald Trump," said Blu. "Weren't you the one screaming about win-win and lose-lose situations in front of that whole crowd of people yesterday? Here's your chance: find your win-win deal where Robert gets to keep his job, but you get

something that will make you happier than you are right now."

Sam threw her arms in the air. "The Art of the Deal!" she screamed. She thrust her hands in her pockets; her left hand hit something hard enough to hurt. "Ow!" She pulled out the cold, metal thing that smashed her fingers. It was Olga's cell phone. Sam had forgotten she still had it. "Oh!" Sam jumped with a thunderbolt of an idea. She turned and ran out of the control room, but stopped at the doorway to spin back around. "Blu," she called out, "you rock!"

As Sam spun back around and out the door, she heard Blu yell, "And don't you forget it!"

CHAPTER 12

Click click click, clack clack click.

This is the morning of Day #3 and I so do not have time to be blogging right now, but I have to tell you what happened last night! It's kind of a long story and I have to pack to catch a plane in one hour, so I'll give you the highlights:

*I have information that proved Robert had lied to my mom.
*I told Robert I had that info (he turned green when he realized I really did have dirt on him) and

would tell my mom unless he did three things:

*Thing 1 – Stop lying to my mom!

*Thing 2 – Stop calling me "Kid"!

*Thing 3 – Let me bring Olga on our trip up
to Toronto!

He said yes to all three things!!!

Okay, I knew he would say yes to Thing 1 because he knows that Mom **hates it** when people tell lies and he's starting to see that she isn't trusting him as completely as she used to. I'm pretty sure that he probably won't keep his promise on Thing 2 for very long, but Olga is coming on our trip! Having my best friend along will make all of the rotten stuff not seem so bad. Olga always makes me laugh. She never makes fun of me, and (best of all at this point in my wacky life) she has this great way of helping me understand why people are treating me so differently now that my sister is famous. All the years we've been friends, I'd never noticed how effortlessly Olga dealt with uncomfortable moments, like people giving her scripts to pass along to her dad the director, or shoving their photos at her in the hope she'd hand them over to her mother's modeling agency. The more I deal with all this phony, famous-life stuff, the more impressed I am by how Olga has handled it without becoming rude or snotty, unlike the living dictionary-definition of rude and snotty, Inga!

Oh! Almost forgot — and this is pretty darn close to the best part — I found out WHY Robert lied to my mom. Ready for this? He had already booked another of his clients (a singer) to do the big football half-time show that Danni is now going to do, but that client *fired* Robert early yesterday morning! Yup, Robert got fired because he'd been spending too much time helping Danni and not enough time helping this other singer! Now, I know it's mean to find joy in another person's problems, but the idea of someone walking over to Mr. Robert Ruebens and telling him that he's fired? I have to admit — I love it! So that's why Danni got the "great gig" at the last minute. When

195

Robert got fired, he canceled the singer's opportunity to do the show. He really is a creep and a half.

I have to finish packing. We are taking a limo over to pick up Olga at her house and then heading to the airport.

The limousine carrying Robert, Rose, Danni, Sam, Michi, Lou, Jean, and Jehan pulled up in front of the beautiful mansion belonging to the Victorio family. Olga was excitedly waiting by the front door. The minute the limo stopped, Olga ran down the steps, dragging her little suitcase.

"Don't leave without saying goodbye!" Mrs. Victorio yelled out of an upstairs window. "We'll be right there."

Sam hopped up to greet her friend. "Isn't this exciting? I'm so happy your parents said yes! Tonight we can stay up late and order room service and play video games on the hotel's TV system! How totally cool is *that*?"

Olga leaned over to whisper, "Listen, Sam, I have to

tell you something. I almost didn't get to come. My mom was totally freaking over the idea of somebody following me around with a video camera. She was afraid I'd say or do something stupid and she'd be humiliated on national TV."

Sam sighed and looked ruefully at the lens of Michi's camera that was pointed at her. "If only my mom could feel the same way."

Olga glanced at her front door to be sure her mother wasn't around before continuing to whisper in Sam's ear. "Maybe if your mom had tripped on a fashion runway and had newspapers all over the world carrying the picture of her flat on the ground, with her underwear hanging out, well, then, maybe she would feel more like mine."

Sam's hand flew to her mouth to hide the giggle that wanted to escape. "Oh, Olga!" she whispered back. "I'd completely forgotten about that!"

Before Olga could respond, her parents and little sister strode out the door and over to the limo. Inga had a wickedly sour look on her face, and even though she seemed to be hiding behind her mother, it was still rather clear that she was upset about something.

Rose popped her head out of the window to say hello to the Victorios. "It's very kind of you to allow Olga to join us," she chimed.

Mrs. Victorio reached out for Olga. She pulled her daughter close, gave her a hug, and whispered in her ear, "Remember what we talked about. I'm very proud of the beautiful person you are inside and out. I know you would never purposely do anything foolish that might embarrass us, but honey, with a video camera on you all the time, you might be tempted to act silly or show off. Be your wonderful self, okay?"

Olga gently pulled away from her mom. "Yes, Mother," she said softly, "don't worry."

Mr. Victorio tossed Olga's little suitcase into the trunk and slammed it shut. "Travel safe and have fun!" he shouted.

"Right," Inga snorted, just loudly enough for everyone to hear, "tons of fun," and marched back into the house.

Sam gave Olga a "what the heck was that all about?" look.

Olga shook her head. "She's so totally jealous; it's killing her that I'm traveling with her newest idol."

Sam giggled. "You mean me?"

Olga laughed out loud. "Yeah, right. You!"

The two girls jumped into the limousine and waved as the car pulled away from the house.

"Honestly, Sam," Olga whispered, "I've never seen Inga so upset. She pitched a massive temper-tantrum and demanded that she be allowed to come. She's going to be watching TV all night and if my face appears on the screen, she might explode with jealousy."

Sam sighed. "So ironic. Here I am desperately dodging the cameras, and your psycho sister is wigging out because she can't get in front of them."

"All right, people," Robert intoned in an obnoxiously loud voice, "for the next twenty-four hours, it is vital that we all stay on schedule. I have a detailed chart that shows where everyone needs to be at all times to make this work." He passed out papers to Rose, Danni, Michi, Lou, Jean, and Jehan.

"Hey," Sam whined, "what about me and Olga?"

"Olga and myself," Robert corrected her. "You don't need a schedule. You need to stay close to your mother when in public and locked in your hotel room at all other times. Now, the adults are going to have an

extraordinarily important meeting, so you and your little friend just sit back and be quiet."

Before Sam could argue with him, Olga whipped out two PSPs from her backpack. Sam grinned as she grabbed one. The two girls snuggled into their corner of the limo and shared a rockin' game of Backyard Basketball.

It was about forty minutes later that the limo pulled into the gated entrance of the hangar where the private plane was waiting for them.

Sam gulped when she saw the little jet. "It's so tiny!" She turned to her mom. "Can that itty-bitty thing really carry all of us? Are you sure this is safe?"

Rose patted her daughter's shoulder and gave a gentle, reassuring laugh. "Of course it's safe, honey." She turned to Robert and quietly asked, "It *is* safe, isn't it?"

Robert was already barking orders into his wrist-phone again. He brushed Rose off with a brusque, "It's fine," and walked away.

Olga had already climbed up the steps and was peeking into the plane. "Come on, Sam!" she called out. "I've flown in one of these before. It's totally safe."

Sam bounced up the steps. She loved what she saw inside. It looked more like a living room than an airplane. Just behind the plane's cockpit, there was a nice table with big, comfy chairs around it. A small kitchen with a microwave was directly in the middle, and the back of the plane had a huge sofa with a giant TV screen hanging on the wall across from it.

The girls ran to the back of the plane to claim the sofa. They buckled their seatbelts and put their feet up on the coffee table just in front of them. Sam picked up a remote control and hit the "on" button. The TV screen lit up and showed options to either watch several movies or play a dozen different video games.

"I have to admit," Sam said to her friend, "this is pretty darn cool."

Click click click, clack clack click.

You are never going to believe this (but I swear I'm telling the truth!!!)! I am writing this from inside a tiny jet airplane that is this very minute flying over the border between the United States and Canada! Seriously! I won't be able to actually

post this to the Web till later, but I really am leaving the US and entering a whole different country! It's funny, from up here, you can't tell where one country ends and the other begins; it just looks like one gigantic, magnificent hunk of land (yeah, I know those are big words, but the view from up here is so amazing that normal, everyday words don't communicate what I'm seeing or feeling).

When we land in Toronto, we have to go through some line where we will show our passports. Yup, Robert's secretary managed to do exactly what King Creepo ordered her to do. You should see which picture they used for me; it's horrible! It's my school photo from last year and you know *nobody* looks good in those. More soon!

The plane landed. Everyone walked off the jet and down a long hallway. At the end of the hallway, a young woman in a very official-looking uniform was looking over people's passports. Before Sam and everyone got close to the young woman, another lady, also in that

official-looking uniform, began running toward them. She looked very angry and was pointing her finger.

"Stop that! Stop that right now!" the woman yelled in a stern voice.

Sam froze; what could she have already done? She braced herself as the woman approached, but then, the woman passed her. Sam let out a relieved breath and looked behind. She noticed that Michi and Lou were videotaping.

"You have to stop that!" The woman planted herself directly in front of Michi's camera. "There is no filming allowed in here!"

Robert strode over and flashed his cheesy white smile. "It's all right. It's all right." He put his hand on the angry woman's shoulder. "I understand you have rules, but I don't think you understand the situation here."

The woman folded her arms and glared at Robert. "I don't understand the *situation*? Please, sir, enlighten me."

Sam's eyes flew open. Couldn't Robert tell that this lady was not kidding around? Didn't he see her official-looking uniform? He'd better watch it; this lady

did not seem the type to give in to Robert's oozy charisma.

Robert took a step back to allow the woman to view him in all his fabulousness. "I am Robert K. Ruebens, music agent to the stars. I'm sure you've heard of me or seen my picture in any number of magazines."

"No, sir," the woman replied flatly.

Robert was visibly startled. "Oh." But he recovered quickly. "Well, I'm sure you've heard of this beautiful young lady. Allow me to introduce to you Miss Danni Devine!"

Robert swept his arm to the side and motioned toward Danni as though she were the blue-ribbon-winning pumpkin pie at a state fair. Danni took the cue and glided over to Robert and the woman.

"Hello." Danni offered her sweetest grin and batted her eyelashes.

The woman remained unimpressed. "There is no filming allowed within a security zone. Please shut off the camera, now."

Robert sidled up to the woman and put his arm around her. "I see where we are having a miscommunication. This," he pointed to the camera,

"is not a film camera, it's a videotape camera. We aren't filming, we are taping."

The woman didn't move a muscle. "Sir, I'm going to ask you politely one more time to shut off the camera."

Robert pulled away and tried to look as impressive as he could. He folded his arms in front of him and glared at the woman with an openly defiant smirk.

"And if I don't have my crew shut off the camera, what are you going to do? Make me eat airplane food?"

The woman kept her eyes on Robert as she pulled a walkie-talkie from her belt. She lifted it to her mouth and quietly said, "Officers, I have a code blue in the corridor."

Suddenly, four incredibly large men, in the same official-looking uniforms, appeared and surrounded Robert. Before anyone could react, the men removed Robert from the hallway, leaving only his briefcase standing in the spot where he had been. Everyone stood completely still until Rose realized that she was in charge. She turned to Michi. "Please refrain from using the camera until we get outside."

Michi nodded and lowered the camera.

"Samantha, would you please pick up and take care of Mr. Ruebens's briefcase for the time being?" Rose posed this as a question, but it was clear from her voice that it was really an order.

Sam ran over and grabbed Robert's briefcase.

Rose turned to the woman. "There, now that that's all taken care of, would you be so kind as to direct us to where we can find our luggage?"

The woman warmly offered to guide Rose and everyone through passport control. She and Rose walked down the hallway together, gabbing away as if they were the best of friends. The woman even took a moment to tell Danni, "I think you are a wonderful performer and my daughter just loves you!"

As they followed close behind, Olga whispered to Sam, "Do you think we'll ever see Robert again?"

Sam tilted her head down and peeked up at Olga with an evil glimmer in her eye. "Not if we get lucky," she said.

Olga had to slam her hands over her mouth to keep from laughing.

Finally the entire group reached the end of the hallway where the young woman was sitting behind a

tall desk, checking everyone's passports. Michi, Lou, Jean, and Jehan all pulled out their passports and walked over to the desk.

Olga pulled her passport out of her purse and waved it in front of her best friend's face. "Here we go, Sam! The last step before we officially enter the country of Canada – passport control! Ready?"

Sam looked over at Danni, who turned to Rose, who stared blankly back at Sam. The Devine women stood awkwardly in their silence, none of them knowing how to proceed.

"Oh, my!" Rose exclaimed. "Robert has our passports! Little Bit," she asked in a shaky voice, "can you please see if Robert put our documents in his briefcase?"

Sam set the briefcase on the ground and opened it. Sure enough, there were the new passports. As she reached to grab them, Sam had a realization that hit her so hard, she felt a physical shock. If she handed the documents to the young woman and said something about these passports being brand-new and less than a day old, then Rose would know that Robert had lied to her and he'd get fired, and Sam would get her normal

life back! Robert would totally get caught and it wouldn't in any way be Sam's fault, so it wouldn't be as if she'd broken her deal with him! This was a total win-win! As Sam pondered her genius scheme, a gigantic smile spread across her face.

"Hey!" Danni barked, snapping Sam out of her private moment. "Whatever this goofy daydream is that's put such a silly grin on your face, could it please wait till later?" Danni held her hand out. "I'm more than a little starving and would like to grab a bite before I go to rehearsal."

Sam stared up at her sister. Even though the tone in Danni's voice had been brusque, there was an obvious twinkle in her eye that revealed how truly excited she was about this trip. Blu's voice rang through Sam's head: "Think about the consequences of your actions. If your mom fires Robert, where does that leave your family?"

A pathetically fake, coughing-like sound came from Olga; it got Sam's attention long enough for the two friends to make eye contact. Olga could tell Sam had latched onto an idea that would cause some amount of trouble and was trying to silently warn Sam not to do whatever she was thinking of doing. Olga's wacky facial

movements did nothing to change Sam's mind – she'd already decided to do the right thing by her family and keep her mouth closed about the passports – but all those tiny muscle ticks and contortions were very entertaining to watch.

Sam snatched up the passports, slammed closed the briefcase, and jumped up. As she raced over to the young woman at the tall desk, Sam whispered to Olga, "Don't look – my picture could destroy your eyeballs."

"It can't be that ba—" Olga started to say, before she saw the terrible photo of Sam. "Oooh! Why did he include *that* photo of you?" she gasped.

Sam grimaced. "Because he likes to see me suffer," she replied sullenly.

Olga and Sam reached the young woman sitting under the "Passport Control" sign.

"Here you go, ma'am," Sam sweetly said as she placed four passports on the tall desk. "Here are the necessary travel documents for myself, my mother, my sister, and my sister's agent. I don't know where the agent is right now; he's the guy your fellow airport security personnel took away for being so unforgivably rude."

Leaning over her tall desk, the young woman

peered down at the nutty little gal waiting for permission to enter the country. Sam looked up and waved, catching the young woman so off guard that she quietly chortled as she sat back in her chair. "Fine then, Miss," she said as she searched the documents for the one with Sam's picture. She found it, and held it up to better study the picture. A sympathetic smile appeared on the young woman's face.

"Yeah." Sam nodded. "I know, it's a seriously awful picture."

The woman tried to be kind. "It certainly doesn't do you justice, but don't worry, I've seen worse." Then she winked at Sam, stamped the inside cover of her passport and handed it back.

A panicked Sam turned to Olga. "Why did she do that? Am I in some kind of trouble?"

Olga handed the young woman her passport as she explained, "Nope, that's what they do. They stamp your passport with the date you entered the country. What's cool is that you then have a kind of souvenir of your trip." The woman stamped the passport and handed it back to Olga, who showed a page to Sam. "See all the different stamps I have? This one is from

Mexico, this one is from Spain, and here's today's stamp from Canada."

Sam put her passport in her pocket. "I'm so glad you came along! You know everything but never make me feel like a loser for not having a clue."

Olga beamed and shyly replied, "I don't know everything. You know a ton of stuff that I don't. Besides, that's what friends are supposed to do, right? Nobody can know everything, so we have lots of friends to fill in all the gaps of the stuff we don't know."

Sam considered Olga's words as she followed everyone over to get their luggage. She'd never thought about friendship like that before. It made a lot of sense. Sam remembered some of the things she'd learned from talking to Blu, especially the stuff he'd told her about fame. That stuff about the TV shows and magazines first talking about you like you're the greatest thing in the world, then getting bored and calling you "so yesterday." Would that happen to Danni? Would people soon get bored with the Devine family and leave them all alone? That would be so awesome! But, then, Danni would be sad. Sam would have to discuss it more with Blu the next chance she got.

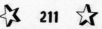 211

Rose made sure everyone had all their bags before they headed toward the final door that led out of the secure area and into the regular part of the airport. Sam suddenly realized how easy everything had been. She had secretly been worried about a mob of people crowding them in, trying to get an autograph or a picture of Danni.

"You know, Mom," she said, "this trip is turning out to be pretty fun."

Rose smiled at Sam as she stepped on the pad on the floor that opened the giant door. As the door opened, flashes of light began to pop so quickly that Sam was blinded. Screaming voices filled the air.

"Danni!"

"Danni Devine!"

"Look over here!"

"Smile for my camera!"

The noise, the people, the crowd – Sam began to feel dizzy. The mass of people that had been waiting behind the door swarmed forward. Sam feared she was about to be crushed. Everything began to get fuzzy and she feared she was going to faint. Suddenly, Robert appeared and grabbed Sam by the arm.

"Danni! Rose! Everyone!" he called out. "Follow me! There's a van waiting at the side door!"

Robert dragged Sam as he blazed a trail through the crowd. He led the party out the door and practically threw each one of them into the car. As they drove off, Sam realized that Robert had saved her from getting trampled by the crowd. She turned to thank him, but his appearance shocked her into silence. Robert was a totally disheveled mess. His tie was undone and hanging around the collar of his half-buttoned shirt that was hanging out of his pants. He was holding his belt, and one pant leg was stuck into his sock.

When Sam finally did find her voice, she had to ask, "What happened to you?"

This comment caused everyone to focus on Robert. They were all just as stunned as Sam.

Robert ground his teeth as he looked away and quietly uttered, "Strip search."

There was a moment of silence in the van before everyone burst out laughing, everyone, that is, expect for Robert. He sulked silently the whole way to the hotel.

Click click click, clack clack click.

It's super-late and I'm supposed to be sleeping (Olga is already snoozing away), so I'm in the bathroom trying to type quietly (it's a good thing this hotel has a wireless connection).

It's the end of Day #3 of my deal with Blu (or early Day #4 because it is 1:30 in the morning).

I don't know where to start. So much happened today. Canada is a really **cool** country (and I don't mean cool as in, I wish I had a sweater). The money is all different colors, everything is written in both English and French, and the people are super-nice.

Once we got to the hotel, Mom left me and Olga to hang out in our suite (yes, a whole big suite just for us!), while Mom and Danni and everyone went to the Skydome to rehearse for Danni's show. The first couple of hours in the hotel were fun. We ate all the candy in the minibar, and played video games on the TV, but then we started to get bored. I called Mom and she arranged for a hotel person to walk us over to the CN Tower. It's the TALLEST building in North America! We took this elevator up and up and up. It went so high that our ears popped! At the top, we walked out onto this deck that had a glass floor. Whoa. I mean, serious *whoa*! Every time I looked down I thought I was going to barf. At first, Olga was laughing at me and my wimpy stomach, but then she started playing along and we were both lying on the glass floor pretending that we were going to barf, when suddenly I hear, *"Samantha Sue"*; Mom and Danni were staring down at me, and I was looking up directly into Michi's video camera.

Olga freaked out that the video of her pretending to barf would be on our TV show and her mother would kill her. She started to cry. I grabbed the earpiece from Michi and spoke to Blu. I begged him to promise not to use the video. At first he got mad and said he couldn't make a promise like that, but as he saw how upset Olga was, he caved in and promised. Whew! If he had used

215

that video, Olga's mom would have NEVER let her hang out with me ever again!

We walked over to the Skydome for Danni's show. If you ever have the chance to go to the Skydome, you really should. It's totally gargantuan and the roof slides back, so it's like being outside when you are really inside! The football game (remember, Danni was here to do the half-time show) was fun, but Danni's show was unbelievable! She sang and danced better than ever. Her dancers were great! The band was perfect! It was one rocking show!

After the show, we went out to dinner. That didn't go so well. We were followed by a bunch of photographers who wouldn't leave us alone. Mom said if we smiled and let them take a few quick pictures and videos outside the restaurant, they'd go away, but it didn't work like that. Not only did they stick around, they snuck into the restaurant and kept flashing their horrible flashes throughout the entire meal. Mom got a headache

from it all. I spilled my soup everywhere because every time I lifted the spoon to my mouth a flash would go off and I'd jump.

Okay, I'm finally getting sleepy and we have to leave super-early tomorrow. So I'll say goodnight and I'll be blogging more ASAP. G'night!

CHAPTER 13

BAM! BAM! BAM!

A terrible pounding on the door awakened Sam. It startled her so much that she forgot where she was and fell out of bed. She stumbled around for a minute until she remembered she was in a hotel and the door to her room was located on the other side of the suite. When she finally got there and opened the door, a very annoyed Robert was standing on the other side.

"Get up!" he barked. "You're the reason we have to leave so early; if I have to be up at this insane hour of the morning, then you do too."

Sam stuck her tongue out at him as he walked away,

but out of the corner of her eye she thought she saw something move. Still with her tongue hanging out, she slowly turned her head.

"Good morning, Michi. Good morning, Lou," she said as unenthusiastically as possible to the video crew taping her from the hallway.

They both waved back with an equal lack of enthusiasm. Sam pulled her tongue back in her mouth and slipped back inside her room. She leaned against the inside of the door and slid down to the floor.

"Who was that?" Olga called out from the bedroom.

"No one special," Sam replied, "just my worst nightmare continuing to follow me throughout my day."

The phone rang and Sam crawled over to the table to answer it.

"Rise and shine, Little Bit! It's Mom. Wakey, wakey! We have an early breakfast meeting and then we need to be wheels up, that's airplane speak for we need to take off, by noon to get you home in time to attend your friend's show."

 219

Sam was still shaking off the morning fuzzies. It took her a moment to remember that the friend her mom was talking about was Mr. Wattabee. Sam groaned when she realized that she really was going to have to attend his silly musical.

"Got it, Mom. I'm awake."

Sam hung up the phone.

"Hey, Olga," she called out, "we need to get ready and get out of here."

Olga walked out of the bedroom fully cleaned up and dressed.

"Wow," said a genuinely impressed Sam, "how'd you do that so fast?"

Olga walked over to the sofa in the center of the living room, grabbed the remote control, and started flipping through the channels.

"I don't know," she said. "But you'd better hurry or they'll send the camera crew in here to document how you brush your teeth."

Sam crawled toward the bathroom. "Oh yeah, that would be pretty. My big old face all covered in toothpaste. That's something I'd want the whole world to see."

She jumped into the shower and was scrubbing the shampoo into her hair when she heard Olga scream. The sound scared Sam so much she almost slipped, but she managed to jump out of the shower, get a towel around her, and rush out to the living room without falling on her face.

"What? What's wrong?" a drippy, soapy Sam panted. "What happened?"

"Look!" Olga was bouncing on the sofa and pointing at the TV.

"Huh?" Sam turned to the giant TV set in time to see Danni, Rose, Sam, and Olga standing in front of the restaurant where they'd had dinner last night.

"That's us!" Sam exclaimed.

"This is CNN, Sam!" Olga cackled with glee. "My sister is going to see this! Me, on TV, with Danni! Ha! Inga is going to be so jealous! I love it! I love it! *I love it!*"

Sam was never the kind of girl to find enjoyment in making someone else feel bad, but Inga really was a spoiled brat. In the four years since Sam and Olga had met at the stables and become best friends, Inga had always looked down on Sam because she never had

cool clothes or did her hair in the latest fashion. The idea of Inga freaking out over something as silly as Olga's being on TV – well, it was the closest thing to poetic justice that Sam could ever have dreamed up. Sam was delighted to see Olga so excited.

Olga was jumping on the sofa, clapping, and laughing out loud, when the door to the girls' suite flew open; Rose came rushing in.

"What in the world is going on in here?" she asked in a worried voice. "Are you both all right?"

Sam was about to answer that they were fine, but she saw Michi and Lou filming the room from the open door. Olga saw them too and did a belly flop from the sofa to the carpet. Sam also hit the floor, trying to hide her messy, wet soapiness from the video camera.

"Mom!" Sam whined at the top of her lungs. "Get out! Get out! I'm in a towel!"

Rose had to work very hard not to chuckle at the scene. "Sorry, Little Bit," she said as she backed out of the room. "Don't get your tail feathers all twisted. We're leaving."

Sam and Olga lay there on the floor next to the sofa without speaking for a full minute before they carefully

 222

lifted themselves just high enough to peek over and be sure that the camera crew was gone. They both let out a sigh of relief.

"You think they got me jumping on the sofa?" Olga asked fearfully.

Sam shook her head. "Nah, you're safe. The camera was focused on my soapy head.

"And I'm sure Blu got a really good laugh out of that one," Sam grumbled to herself as she headed back to the bathroom to get the shampoo out of her hair.

Click click click, clack clack click.

OH! OH! OH! SO much to tell you! I need to slow down or I'll forget something. (Huge calming breath.) Okay, I'm better. Here goes:

Right now, I'm back on the itty-bitty airplane flying home from our unbelievable trip to Toronto, Canada. It is currently the middle of Day #4 of my 5-day deal with Blu.

This morning, we left the hotel to have a

breakfast meeting with a Canadian TV producer who is thinking about creating a whole Christmas television special around Danni, and of course, he wants me and Mom to be on the show as well (grrrr). We got to the restaurant a little early, and as it turns out, we were **too** early. Seems the producer had a meeting with someone else before us.

We walk up to the table and the producer is talking to a pretty girl. When the girl saw Robert, she stood up, threw her napkin on the table, and proceeded to yell at Robert. Yes, she screamed at Robert! Get this; the girl is a singer and dancer like Danni. It turns out that SHE was the client who fired Robert for not taking care of her career and that's why Danni got the job doing the half-time show at the Skydome (remember, I blogged about all that). The producer was thinking about using either Danni or this other girl for his TV special. So, there is Robert, getting bawled out for being a rotten agent, in front of everybody, and my mom and Danni finally find out the real reason

Danni got the half-time-show job at the last minute.

The girl finished screaming at Robert and stormed off. Then my mom began to yell at Robert for lying to her and Danni! It was *awesome*! Mom totally ripped into him! She called him a creep, a liar, and (my favorite) a *scoundrel* (isn't that a great word?)! She went as far as to tell him that from now on he has to include her in all negotiations for Danni (no more making decisions and telling Mom about them afterward) and that if she ever catches him in a lie again, he will be fired on the spot! *Seriously!* Robert was stunned. He tried to stammer out some kind of lame apology, but Mom cut him off and told him to "zip it"! She really said that! LOL! It was beautiful!

Then, Mom makes a very gracious apology to the producer, sits down, and takes control of the meeting. *Robert didn't utter a peep!* Mom negotiated the deal for the Christmas special and

 225

managed to get Danni even more money than the producer had originally offered. She can get a little nutty sometimes, but when my mom pulls it together, she is amazing!

So we finish the meeting and the producer leaves. We prepare to exit the restaurant and Robert makes this big show out of taking out his wallet to pay for breakfast, as if he were the "man" of our family (yech). He hands the lady a 100 dollar bill and smugly tells her to keep the change. She looks at him and says that's very kind, but seeing as the money isn't worth anything to her, she'd prefer he use something of real value instead. Robert turns all purple and loudly asks the lady when 100 dollar bills stopped being legal currency. She stares at him as if he were a bug on her windshield and replies, "American 100 dollar bills stopped being legal currency when you entered the COUNTRY OF CANADA. We use our own money up here, sir."

I began laughing so hard I thought my brains would get squished right out of my ears! She said the word "sir" in such a way that everyone in the whole place realized she was really saying, "giant doofus-head." Robert knew that she was completely correct; his face went from *perturbed purple* to *mortified maroon* in, like, ten seconds. He fished a bunch more bills out of his pocket, found a Canadian $100, and left it on the table without another word.

Best part of everything???? It was all caught on tape by Michi and Lou!!!
:-)

Bye – or should I say *Au Revoir* (remember, they speak both English **and** French up here).

The limousine pulled up in front of the Victorios' home. Sam and Olga hopped out as Mrs. Victorio and Inga walked out of the house.

"Welcome home, my little world traveler!" Mrs. Victorio called out.

Olga cringed. "Hi, Mom."

Sam quietly giggled to her friend, "Little world traveler. That's so cute."

Olga turned her head so her mother couldn't see and quickly stuck her tongue out at Sam.

Sam giggled even harder. "Keep it up and I'll get the camera crew out here."

Olga's tongue swiftly slipped back inside her mouth.

Rose stepped out of the limo to greet Olga's mom.

"You have a very well-behaved daughter, Giselle. She is welcome to travel with us anytime."

Sam could tell this compliment pleased Mrs. Victorio. *Cool beans*, she thought to herself, *this means I'll be able to bring Olga along on future trips!*

"In fact," Rose continued, "if you don't mind, we'd like to invite Olga to join us for dinner and a show tonight."

Sam caught her breath so fast she almost gagged. She began coughing wildly. Everyone stared at her.

"You all right, Sam?" a worried Rose asked.

"Mom," a shaky Sam struggled to respond, "what do you mean, 'join us for dinner and a show'? I'm the one who made the promise to my fr– fr– friend." Sam

stumbled over actually calling Mr. Wannabee a friend.

Rose walked over and put her arm around her daughter. "Oh, come on, Samantha, we've had such a wonderful weekend together as a family that I hate to see it end. You were willing to come to Canada to see Danni, so Danni and I would be proud to accompany you to your friend's show." Rose turned and looked into the limo, directly at Danni, who had been lost in her own thoughts. "Isn't that right, Danielle Ann?"

It took a minute, but Danni recognized that her mother wasn't really asking a question. "Yeah, it's cool. Love to go with you tonight, Little Bit."

Panic bells were going off in Sam's head. *This can't happen. The stables are my last refuge. I have to keep my family and the camera crew away.*

Olga gave Sam a confused look. Sam hadn't said anything to her about a friend being in a show. Olga mouthed silently, "What friend?" to Sam. Sam put her hand under her nose so Rose couldn't see, and mouthed back the words "Mister Wannabee," for Olga's eyes only. It took Olga a moment to understand, but when she did, she gasped in horror. Sam gave a quick nod and looked up to Rose.

 229

"Yeah, but Mom, it's not a big deal. It's just a friend in a silly little musical. Really, you'll be bored to tears."

Rose hugged Sam and smiled. "Oh, Sweetie, don't you worry about your old mom. I'm having such a lovely time hanging out with my girls, I can't bear to let it end."

"Seriously, Mom," Sam stammered, "you and Danni must be exhausted after that long airplane ride. Don't you just want to go home and rest?"

Danni popped her head out the window of the limo. "I'm actually still pretty pumped up from the great show last night," she happily chirped. "I'm up for dinner and a show."

Suddenly Inga jumped into the conversation. "Mother," she whined, "Olga just got home and already she gets to go out again? That's not fair! I miss her when she's gone and now she's going out to dinner *and* to a show?"

Olga and Sam turned to each other with utter shock on their faces. What in the world was happening?

Inga continued, "If Olga goes out I will be home alone and I'll be missing her *so much*!"

Rose smiled. "I just had the most brilliant idea! Inga, why don't you join us?" Sam and Olga's shared shock turned to mutual disgust. Spoiled-rotten Inga had just tricked Rose into inviting her along so the little rat could hang out with Danni. Having dinner with Danni Devine would give Inga plenty to brag about with her other snotty little friends.

Mrs. Victorio clasped her hands in front of her and grinned. "Thank you, Rose. What a wonderful idea. Girls," she looked at Olga and Inga, "why don't you run upstairs and get cleaned up?" She turned back to Rose. "How about I drop them off at whatever restaurant you choose, that way you'll have time to clean up as well?"

Inga batted her eyelashes and tipped her head to make sure she looked as adorable as possible. "Maybe, if it's all right with Mrs. Devine and Danni, maybe we could go to the Rainforest Café? They have super-yummy food and I like looking at all the paintings of the animals on the walls."

Danni smiled at Inga. "What a great idea! I'm up for it!"

Rose threw open her arms. "Then it's settled. We'll

meet at the Rainforest Café at 5:30. That will allow us plenty of time to get to the show."

Sam and Olga shared one last look; dread was written all over both of their faces.

The whole way home, throughout her shower, and as they drove to the restaurant, Sam couldn't shake off the bad feelings that were swimming in the pit of her stomach. She didn't trust Inga; she knew the little faker had to have some plan in her evil little mind to make herself the focus of the evening. *I bet she spends the whole night with her face in Michi's camera*, Sam thought to herself.

The limo carrying Rose, Danni, and Sam pulled up in front of the restaurant, directly behind Mrs. Victorio's car. Olga and Inga got out to meet them. Inga was dressed in the trendiest, most glittery outfit Sam had ever seen.

"Where'd she get the costume?" Sam whispered to Olga.

"You don't know the half of it," her friend answered back. "Miss Thing tried on ten different outfits before deciding on that one. She is determined to be the star tonight."

Inga planted herself next to Danni. "Gosh, Danni," she gushed, "you look hot! I love your hair and your makeup! I hope I'm as beautiful as you when I grow up!"

Danni basked in the adoration of her young fan. "Why, thank you, Inga."

Rose looked at the large number of people standing in front of the café. "Goodness," she said, "it's been so long since we've been out in public without Robert. I guess I'll have to go fight that crowd to get us a table. You all wait here and, please, stick together."

Two young girls gingerly approached Danni.

"Excuse me," the taller of the two shyly asked, "are you Danni Devine?"

"Yes, she is," Inga loudly and proudly announced.

"I knew it!" the smaller girl squealed. "Would you please sign my T-shirt? I love your songs! Please? I'll never wash this shirt!"

"Sure," Danni softly replied, "I'd be happy to, but let's keep it quiet. I don't want to attract a lot of attention. I'm trying to be low-key."

"Sure. Yeah. We understand." Both girls nodded with enormous smiles.

Inga seemed bothered about something. She turned

her head from side to side as if she was searching for someone.

"What's the matter with her?" Sam asked Olga.

Olga shrugged. "Who knows? She's probably annoyed that no one has asked for *her* autograph."

Rose reappeared. She held out a small square object that looked like a plastic waffle. "They think they'll have a table for us in about fifteen minutes," she explained, "but I'm not so sure. I see a lot of people holding these table beepers."

"I love those things," said Olga. "They light up when your table is ready."

Inga was bewildered. "But didn't you tell them about Danni? I can't believe they'd make a star wait for a table!"

Rose spoke sternly. "Inga, we do not take advantage of Danni's position like that. It's not nice and it's not fair."

Sam was impressed. Maybe her mom had a better grip on this whole fame situation than she'd thought. Sam turned to see if Danni had taken note of how Rose had handled Inga's bratty moment, but Danni's attention was elsewhere. She was carefully eyeing a group of teenagers who were looking and pointing at her.

"I don't like standing out here in the open. I'm afraid I'm going to get recognized by everyone and trapped in a mob. Sam," she asked as sweetly as she could, "would you please go find somebody else holding a table pager thingy like this and see if they'll trade with us?"

"What?" Sam couldn't believe her sister was being so childish. "Nobody is going to trade pagers for no reason."

"Sam has a point," Rose agreed. She opened her purse and pulled out a fifty-dollar bill. "Here," she handed it to Sam. "If you ask kindly, explain we are in a terrible hurry and offer them this, I'm sure you'll find some kind-hearted person who'll let us take their table."

Sam looked at the growing number of people hanging around the restaurant. "Don't make me do this," she griped. "I don't know what to say."

Danni shot her sister a sharp look. "It's not that big a deal. You find a person holding one of those things and ask how long they have to wait. If it's more than

fifteen minutes, you say, 'thank you' and walk away. If it's less than fifteen minutes," Danni grabbed the money and put it in Sam's hand, "you say what Mom just said and give them the fifty bucks. It's not brain surgery."

Sam grimaced, but she turned and walked toward the crowd. She focused on what people were holding. She saw a couple of purses and a few cell phones. Sam spun back around to yell to her mom that this plan wasn't going to work, but she saw that Danni was getting more and more nervous. Sam knew she had to keep looking. Finally she saw another pager thingy; she weaved and bobbed and fought her way through the crowd until she finally reached the person with the pager.

"Excuse me, please," asked the flushed and flustered Sam, looking into the eyes of an annoyed-looking woman. "Um…I'm supposed to ask you about your *wait*," Sam blurted.

The woman stared down at Sam. "What did you ask me?"

Sam figured that the woman must have trouble hearing, so she repeated more loudly, "I'm supposed to ask you about your wait."

The woman holding the pager turned deep red and yelled in an ear-splitting voice, "I have never been so insulted in all my life! How dare you? Who do you think you are?"

Everyone in the crowd went silent. The stillness around her was painful; Sam stood frozen to her spot. She looked up at the woman with pure confusion. "I don't…what did…see, my sister there," Sam pointed back at Danni, "my sister told me to ask, and give you this money."

The woman scowled, pushed Sam aside, and began to march toward Danni. It was only then that Sam realized the lady was a large person. She was a very large person; in fact, she was a super-duper fat person. It hit Sam like a ton of bricks; when she'd asked the lady about her "wait," the lady thought she'd been asking about her "weight"!

The mess that followed happened in an instant, but to Sam, it felt as if everything was happening in slow motion.

The woman ranted and flailed her arms wildly as she got in Danni's face. Danni tried to stammer out an apology, but she couldn't be heard over the woman's

shrieking. Out of nowhere, a minivan pulled up at the curb and three men jumped out. Two of the men had picture cameras and the third man held a video camera. They began endlessly snapping pictures and yelling.

"Danni," one photographer hollered, "smile for my camera!"

"What d'you do to this poor lady?" the guy with the video camera shouted.

"It's the paparazzi!" Rose shrieked as she tried to maneuver herself in-between Danni and the camera. "Run, Danni! Get out of here!"

Danni was so distressed by the chaos, the flashing lights, and the screaming, that she couldn't move. Rose was swinging her purse at the cameras and yelling, "Get out of here! Leave us alone!"

Inga also jumped in front of Danni, but instead of shooing away the photographers she posed for them.

Sam ran over to try to help. "Leave my sister alone! This is all a misunderstanding! Please, everyone, stop!"

Olga grabbed Inga and pulled her away from the cameras, but Inga became angry and tried to wrestle away.

"Knock it off!" she cried as she wiggled free of Olga's grasp. "This is my turn! Don't ruin it for me! They won't be here very long."

"How do you know the paparazzi won't be here very long?" Olga asked suspiciously. "Did you have something to do with this, Inga? *Did* you?"

The expression on Inga's face was a strange mix of desperation and arrogance. "You got to be on TV last night *and* this morning! It's only fair *I* get to be on TV tonight!"

Olga tightened her grip on her little sister. "When we get home, I'm telling Mom and Dad that you called the paparazzi and told them where to find us, and you will be grounded for the rest of your life!" She dragged Inga over to the side of the melee, out of camera range.

Rose continued swatting at the cameras with her purse, Sam was jumping up and down to block their view of Danni, and the fat lady was still screaming. Nobody noticed the Jeep pull up in front of the minivan. Robert leaped out of the driver's seat and pushed his way through the tangle of people until he reached Danni.

"Come on!" he roared as he yanked Danni's arm.

"Rose! Sam! Girls! Move it!"

Robert practically tossed Danni into the back of the Jeep, where she landed on Michi. Rose hopped into the passenger seat and pulled Sam onto her lap. Lou reached out and lifted Olga and Inga into the tiny bit of open space left in the back.

"Hang on!" Robert hit the gas pedal so hard that the Jeep left skid marks as it blazed out of the parking lot and away from the nightmarish scene.

Nobody said a word. When they reached the Victorios' house, Inga raced inside before anyone could say anything to her. Olga stepped out of the Jeep and turned to give Sam a sad little wave goodbye before heading in to find her parents and tell them about the disaster Inga had caused.

When the Jeep stopped in front of the Devines' home, everyone continued to sit silently. It was Rose who finally spoke.

"Robert," she said carefully, "I want you to know I'm still very angry with you; your lying to us about Danni's Canada job and the whole TV show for that matter is utterly unacceptable." She paused a minute to find the perfect words to express her feelings.

"However, tonight, you," Rose looked back at the camera crew, "and you as well, Michi and Lou, you all did a wonderful thing, swooping in to rescue us from that terrible situation. You didn't have to do it, but you did, and I am immeasurably grateful."

Rose stepped onto the driveway and reached out to guide Danni, whose face was completely covered in tear stains and runny mascara. Mother and daughter put their arms around each other as they gingerly walked up the steps and through the front door.

Sam watched her mom and sister. *What a freaky twenty-four hours*, she thought, *Mom finally stands up and takes control of Danni's career, Inga the brat turns into a rat, and Robert becomes the hero*. She sighed and looked up to see Robert staring at her through the rear-view mirror.

"Well?" he inquired.

Sam didn't understand. "Well, what?"

"Well," Robert explained, sounding as annoyed with her as usual, "unless you plan on sleeping here, I'd suggest you get out of the car. Hmm?"

Sam chuckled. *There we go*, she thought, *everything is back to normal*.

241

Lou assisted Sam as she climbed out the back of the Jeep. She took one step toward the house, but turned back quickly.

"Robert, wait! There's something I don't understand. How did you know that we were in trouble?"

Without looking at her, he replied, "Kid, I know all. I see all."

Sam stuck her tongue out at him as the Jeep began to pull away, but Michi's snapping fingers snagged her attention. Sam looked up in time to see Michi silently mouthing the word "Blu" as the Jeep disappeared around the side of the mansion.

Sam ran up to her room and pounded on the mirror.

"Blu," she called out, "Blu! Let me in!"

But there was no response. Sam looked at the clock on her desk; it was seven forty-five. Blu must have already gone home for the night. Wait! *Seven forty-five?* Sam slapped her hand to her head. Mr. Wannabee's show! She was late! There was no time to find her mom, and anyway, Sam didn't want her tagging along. She grabbed a piece of paper, scribbled a note explaining to her mom that she'd taken her bike over to

242

see her friend's show, and raced out of her room.

Sam pedaled with all her might; she didn't want to arrive late and make a spectacle of herself trying to find a seat when the show had already started. Luckily, she reached the theater, locked up her bike, ran inside, and handed her ticket to an usher, with less than a minute to spare. Unfortunately, the usher walked her into the packed auditorium, down to the very first row. He pointed to four empty seats that were smack-dab in the middle of that row. In fact, they were smack-dab in the middle of the entire theater!

"Pardon me, sir," Sam whispered as politely as possible while still gasping for air from her insanely fast bike ride. "Could you please put me somewhere that's not, you know, practically *on* the stage?" She tried to smile and bat her eyelashes the way Danni had done when she'd wanted to charm that security-officer-lady in Canada. "I came to *see* the show, not be in it."

The usher ignored Sam's attempt at adorableness. He scowled as he quickly glanced around the theater; then, he stuck out his lower lip, shook his head, handed Sam back her ticket, and walked away.

Sam sighed as she looked across the row of already

comfortably seated people she was going to have to squeeze past to reach her now officially designated perch. *How come that cute thing always works for Danni, but never for me?* she wondered while working her way across the crowd. "Excuse me. I'm so sorry. Excuse me," she said over and over as she accidentally tripped and tramped on everyone's toes.

Finally, she reached her seat and slid into it as the lights began to dim. *Okay*, she thought, *I made it. Now all I need to do is suffer through Mr. Wannabee's performance and pop backstage to prove to him that I kept my word. Then, I can go home, pull the blankets over my head and dream about tomorrow when I will wake up, tell Blu I don't want to do his stupid TV show, and get my normal, boring life back!*

Sam yawned. She hadn't realized she was so exhausted, but this moment of quiet sitting was relaxing; her eyelids suddenly felt very heavy. For a single second, Sam was on the verge of falling asleep, but the first blast of music from the orchestra, located directly in front of her, was so unbelievably loud and startling, she jolted straight up and almost jumped out of her seat.

Sam had expected to be completely and utterly bored by *"My Fair Lady"* because it was an old musical about some girl living in England about a hundred years ago. How could something so removed from Sam's own life be interesting? Yet, over the course of the next seventy-five minutes, a remarkable thing happened; as the music played and the performers sang and danced, Sam began to enjoy the performance. She laughed at the jokes. She took in the beautiful colors and fabrics of the costumes. Her head bounced along to the beat of the songs. She cringed as the *"Fair Lady"* said and did stuff that the other, more educated and cultured characters found to be uncivilized and uncouth. Sam even stopped seeing Mr. Wattabee as the grumpy guy from the stables and truly saw him as the snooty Professor Higgins. Sam began to see parallels between her own life and that of the *"Fair Lady"* in how everyone else seemed to want to change the outside of the person – clothes, behavior, speech – to better fit what *they* wanted, yet they seemed to forget about the inside of the person – how she felt, what she thought. When the curtain came down at the end of the show, Sam was the first one to applaud! She couldn't believe

how much she'd loved the show! She was almost sorry that she hadn't brought Rose and Danni along: not only would they have enjoyed it themselves, but Sam would have had somebody to discuss the show with!

Trapped by the crowd, Sam had to wait to get out of her seat. She was genuinely excited to tell Mr. Wattabee how much she'd appreciated both the whole show and his performance.

When she did eventually wind her way through to the backstage area, Sam couldn't locate Mr. Wattabee. There were too many people. Sam found herself squished into a corner of the room. After getting elbowed in the head for the fourth time, she climbed up on a stool to try to see over the crowd. She carefully balanced both feet on the top of the stool and slowly lifted her torso.

"Devine!" Mr. Wattabee's all-too familiar voice rang out.

Sam tried to turn toward the part of the room where she thought she'd heard that voice, but lost her balance and tumbled off the stool. As she was falling, she closed her eyes and braced her body for the imminent pain of hitting the ground. Instead of the hard, cool slam of the

floor, Sam was surprised to encounter the warm, safe feeling of a person's arms. Sam opened her eyes and was stunned to see that *Blu* had caught her!

"What are you doing here?" she asked.

"Saving your silly self," he replied with a stern glare. Blu set Sam down, put his fists on his hips, and fiercely stared down at the shaky girl.

"Have you completely lost your mind? Riding your bike alone, *at night*?" Blu was so angry he was spitting out his words. "What kind of brainless bonehead rides her bicycle halfway across town in the dark? What were you thinking?"

Sam couldn't give Blu an answer. Her mind was still trying to figure out how circumstances had changed so quickly: one minute she was doing a header off a stool, and the next, Blu was bawling her out!

"Wait a minute! Wait a minute!" she barked back. "How did you know...what in the world are you doing here?"

Blu threw his hands in the air. "There I was, minding my own business, eating my dinner, and putting the finishing touches to the first episode of your family's TV show from the crew house in the backyard, when what do I see from one of the live-feed monitors? I see you scrawling something on a scrap of paper and running out of the house – *alone* – at *night*! I'm thinking you've snapped and are running away! So, I zoom in the camera lens to read your note and discover that while you haven't taken off to join the circus, you've decided to attend the theater – *alone* – at *night*!" Blu's tone went from angry to sarcastic. "Thanks so much for not mentioning which theater you were riding off to. I only frittered away an entire tank of gasoline driving from one end of this city to the other looking for you."

Sam knew she was supposed to feel awful about causing Blu to waste his time and his gas looking for her, but she was still consumed with confusion.

"But, *why*?" she cried out. "Why have you been out looking for me? I'm not your responsibility!"

"No, Nutjob!" Blu spluttered. "You are not my *responsibility*, but you are my *friend*!" His voice softened. "And I don't let my friends put themselves in harm's way. Go get your bike. I'll follow you home in my car."

The clear understanding that Blu considered her

a true friend was so overwhelming, it made Sam feel giddy. Suddenly, she was overtaken by an uncontrollable fit of the giggles.

Blu was not amused. "Don't you go all crazy on me." His tone was still terse, but the edges of his mouth began to twitch just enough to allow for a barely visible hint of a smile. "I'm tired. I'm hungry, and I'm more than a little cranky. Move it."

"Okay." Sam nodded. "But first I have to congratulate Mr. Wanna—" Sam caught herself. "*Wattabee*. I have to congratulate Mr. Wattabee on his great performance tonight."

Blu gritted his teeth and let out an audible, "grrrrrrrrrrrrrrrrr," but he did agree. "Yeah, it's the right thing to do. Go ahead, but make it fast. My dinner is getting colder by the moment and my mood isn't doing much better."

Sam jolted her arms forward to give Blu two big, fast thumbs ups, before turning and pushing her way through the crowd over to where Mr. Wattabee was standing.

"Devine!" Mr. Wattabee bellowed as he saw her approaching. "I'm so thrilled to see you! Thank you for coming tonight! Everyone," he shouted with enthusiasm, "we have a VIP honoring us with her presence. Please say hello to Miss Samantha Devine!"

All the people in the room cheered and welcomed Sam, who was positively beaming. She couldn't believe how awesome this evening had turned out. She'd gotten to see a great show, was made to feel totally special by Blu, and now, Mr. Wattabee was treating her as his most treasured guest of honor. It was the first time in four miserable days that Sam had actually relaxed.

"You were awesome in the show, sir," Sam gushed. "Seriously! I loved it! I had no idea you were such a talented actor! Thank you so much for giving me a ticket! I had the best time and can't wait to tell everyone to come and see your show!"

Mr. Wattabee was smiling and nodding, but it seemed as if he wasn't really listening to Sam. "Now," he clapped his hands together and rubbed them in anticipation. "Where is that sister of yours? What did she think of the show?"

"I'm sorry, but my sister couldn't make it."

Mr. Wattabee's smile dropped from his face. "What?"

"Yeah." Sam didn't like the way the energy of the room was changing. Just a second ago, everything had felt nice and cozy; suddenly a cold front had swept in. "She really wanted to come tonight, but, you see, we just got back from Canada and had an insanely awful dinner, and so she had to go home. But I'm here! I loved the show! Did I tell you how amazing I thought you were?"

The entire backstage area had gone silent. Mr. Wattabee's expression was a strange mix of annoyance and crushing disappointment. He rubbed his forehead as if to erase some terrible pain. "This is our last night, Devine," he said in a quivering voice. "I told you that. I told you Sunday is our last show. You promised you'd bring your sister. I told everyone that Danni Devine would be attending our last performance."

"Oh, Mr. Wattabee, I didn't promise to bring Danni!" Sam began to panic. She knew she hadn't made any kind of promise like that because she never would, but if Mr. Wattabee believed that she had, then he would be so mad at her that he'd make life at the stables unbelievably, unfathomably and unimaginably horrible. "I'm super-seriously sorry if you thought

that's what I said. I can't *make* my sister do anything. I can't make promises for her. I promised *I'd* come, and I did!"

Mr. Wattabee wasn't looking at Sam anymore. His eyes were focused on the floor, but Sam could see that all the other actors in the room were glaring at him with open displeasure. *They're mad at him*, she thought. He'd promised them all a chance to perform for a famous singer, and now he looks like a liar.

"Your show rocked, Mr. Wattabee!" Sam tried desperately to salvage the situation. "It *wickedly* rocked! I've never enjoyed a show as much in my entire life! I'm going to tell everyone I know how great the show was and do my best to get them all to come to your next one!"

"There isn't going to be a next one," Mr. Wattabee growled. "Our little opera company hasn't been able to sell enough tickets to pay for the rental of this auditorium. I thought that if your sister came tonight, we could get some solid publicity out of her visit. With that publicity, we could maybe get the owner of this theater to give us a break and let us put on one more show. Do you see how it works, Devine? We are desperate to get people to come and see our little shows; we can't afford to put big, splashy ads in the newspapers. Your sister blows her nose and it's on TV all over the world! We were counting on your sister to help us!" Mr. Wattabee looked Sam squarely in the eye. "*I* was counting on *you*."

Even though the following fifteen seconds were deadly quiet, Sam's heart was beating so forcefully, she thought everyone could hear it. The painful stillness was finally broken when someone standing behind Mr. Wattabee asked a question; the voice of the person asking that question was low, steady, and way too calm.

"I came in a bit late, and only got part of the conversation, so, would you all please allow me the opportunity to sum up what I believe I've just heard?"

Mr. Wattabee spun around and gasped. As he turned, Sam caught a glimpse of the person behind him, and she gasped too. In fact, pretty much everyone in the room let out a loud gasp as they recognized the one and only Miss Danni Devine, standing in the doorway.

CHAPTER 14

Click click click, clack clack click.

Good morning and welcome to Day #5 of my deal with Blu. Before I explain what I'm thinking about my future (the TV show thing, I mean) I **HAVE** to tell you what happened last night.

I made it to Mr. Wannabee's show. It was super-brilliantly good! Seriously!

After the show, I stick around to congratulate Mr. Wannabee. When he first sees me, he's all happy

that I came, but then he asks if I brought Danni along. I didn't want to go into all the details of our evening (getting attacked by an angry obese lady and ambushed by photographers isn't easy to explain), so I said that Danni wanted to come but couldn't (considering how she felt by the time we got home, it wasn't too much of a fib).

Mr. Wannabee's mood completely changed. He freaked out on me because he'd promised people that Danni would be at the show, and he'd hoped to get some publicity out of Danni's visit (apparently the light opera company hasn't been making much money). He blamed **me** for ruining his night and his light opera company! So, you have to imagine the setting: I'm in a room full of people who don't even know me, but they all now **HATE** me. I'm the evil girl who didn't follow through on her promise (a promise I swear I never made!!), and thus has ruined their chance to keep their little theater group alive. This was not exactly a friendly crowd to be stuck in.

I didn't know what to do. I thought about running out of the room, but Blu was there (that's a long story for another blog) and I didn't want to look like a giant chicken in front of him. Heck, I said I was sorry! What more did they want? Besides, how can you be mad at a person for not following through on a plan she didn't even know about?!?!

Here comes the most awesome part of the night. Danni and my mom show up! Yup! See, I'd left a note telling my mom that I'd gone to see Mr. Wannabee's show. She found the note and went ballistic that I'd gone out alone at night. Mom was rushing out the door to go find me, when Danni asked where she was going. Mom showed her the note. Danni tried to get Mom to chill, but that made Mom even madder! Mom told Danni that it was **their** fault that I'd gone out alone, that by first agreeing to go to the show, and then forgetting all about it, they had put me in a lose-lose position. And – get this part – **Danni agreed with Mom!** I can't believe it! Danni said it was their

bugging-out on their promise that forced me to do what I did (I still don't think riding my bike at night is that big a deal, but apparently everyone else does!).

So, I'm in that backstage area, feeling like the worst person on the planet (or at least in the theater) because Mr. Wannabee is accusing me of ruining his theater group, when Mom and Danni walk in. Mom begins to rip into old Mr. Wannabee the way a hungry kid rips into a bag of cookies – with gusto! She tells him how wrong he was to have expected so much from a young woman (a young woman!) without having the guts to explain what was really happening. Mind you, Mom did this all without yelling or carrying on like a fool. Rose Devine is one cool cat when she wants to be!

There's more! Mr. Wannabee apologizes as if his life depends on it! He must have said, "I'm sorry" at least a million different ways. Then, Danni walks over and asks him if the light opera

257

company is really **THAT** important to him. He practically starts crying and explains that it's the most important thing in his life! She listens, nods, and tells him she can understand because that's how important the horses are to me, and she would appreciate it if he would be nicer to me when I go to the stables. Okay, now I'm about to cry; all this time, I never thought Danni realized just how much I love riding, and there she is explaining my passion to others and working to make my life a little easier. Danni offers Mr. Wannabee a deal: she'll let him take her picture and use it for publicity purposes *if* he promises to stop treating me like a second-class citizen. I'm so excited at this point I can barely breathe, *but there's even more*! Mr. Wannabee not only accepts Danni's deal — he suggests I switch my job from pooper-scooper to walker! That means instead of mucking the stalls, I get to be the person who goes and gets the horses for the riders and walks them from the pasture to the barn where they get saddled. It's a dream job!

I looked over at my mom and clasped my hands together to silently beg her to let me do this. Mom smiled and nodded. Danni waved her hand to catch my eye. She gave me a look to ask if this was what I wanted. I smiled so hard I thought my face would fall off. Danni shook Mr. Wannabee's hand, and I nearly exploded with happiness!

Michi and Lou had, of course, followed Mom and Danni backstage, so they volunteered to shoot some tape of Danni talking to the members of the opera company and then send the video to all the news and paparazzi outlets. They guaranteed the footage would garner a ton of publicity for the group.

I looked around for Blu to see what he thought of everything that had happened, but he had vanished. I guess once he saw my mom show up, he knew he didn't have to worry about me anymore. I hope his dinner wasn't too cold by the time he got back to finishing it.

One more thing about last night, Lou tied my bike to the back of the Jeep and drove us home. On the way, Danni leaned over and gave me a little peck on the cheek. I asked her what it was for. She told me that I had helped her learn a major lesson – that being famous and counting on your fans to show up and support your dreams means that you need to be willing to give back by showing up to support other peoples' dreams. Just because the thing somebody desires doesn't involve being on TV or making tons of money, doesn't make it any less real or important.

I don't think I've said this in a while, but I don't just love my sister because she's my sister, I really like her, too!

So now I have to deal with Blu and our agreement. Honestly, I don't know what I'm going to tell him. I have to admit I've enjoyed having him around and feeling like I had somebody who was totally on my side, watching out for me; but still, I can't imagine living with all the craziness that comes with having TV cameras in my face day and night. I can't wait to see the first episode of our show (*The Devine Life*). I trust that Blu won't make us all look stupid, but then again, when you give somebody the freedom to show bits and pieces of your life, you can never be sure how it's going to look to the rest of the world.

Sam knocked on the mirror, but like the night before, Blu didn't answer. Sam felt irritated. Where was he? The editing of the show should be done by now! Had he decided that Sam and her family were too much trouble? Had last night pushed him over the edge? Had he bailed on the gig without telling her?

Sam was silent as she walked downstairs, entered the dining room, and ate her breakfast. She was so lost in her thoughts that she barely acknowledged her mom or sister. She even ignored a snotty comment from Robert.

Rose whispered into Danni's ear, "Do you know what's going on with Sam?"

Danni shook her head and shrugged her shoulders.

Rose leaned over and checked Sam's forehead for a fever, three times. She got up from the table and stood back to take a good, long look at her sullen daughter.

"Robert? Danni? Would you give Sam and me a moment for a private discussion?"

"Mom," Sam whimpered as she watched her sister and Robert bolt out of the room, "I'm fine. Please don't make a big deal out of this. I just happen to have a lot on my mind."

Rose sat down across from Sam. She took in a deep breath and prepared to speak, but she couldn't figure out what to say, so she ended up doing nothing more than exhaling loudly.

"And you think there's something wrong with me?" Sam cracked. "You sure you're okay, Mom?"

The question surprised Rose. "Me? I'm fine. I'm trying to make sure *you're* all right."

Sam's response came out a little crankier than she meant it to. "I told you I'm fine. I'm deep in thought, that's all."

Rose dipped her head forward and closed her eyes. Sam worried that she'd hurt her mother's feelings and was about to apologize, but Rose spoke first. "Sweetie, there's something you need to know."

Sam immediately wished she could rewind the entire morning. Any conversation that starts with a parent saying, "there's something you need to know" never ends well. On TV, this would be where the daughter finds out she's really a robot, or her mom is really a robot, but this wasn't TV, it was Sam's real life. Of course, her real life was being put on TV, so anything was possible. Sam shook her head to erase all the wacky thoughts and give her full attention to her mom.

Rose's words tumbled out so quickly it was hard to tell where one word stopped and the next one started. "Samantha, I know you hate the idea of living inside a TV show, but I also know you love the stables, and I wanted you to be close to the stables because you've been wonderful about making so many sacrifices this past year and allowing Danni to be a star and you've never complained and so I was willing to agree to almost anything to get you a house near your horses, and because of that I signed the stupid papers and if you want out we can quit, but then we'll have to move because we don't actually own this house, yet."

Rose stopped to breathe; this gave Sam a moment to absorb everything she'd just had thrown at her.

"Yet?" she asked. "What do you mean, yet?"

"The deal with the network is that if we agree to live in this house and allow our lives to be taped for the TV show for three years, then along with all the money they are paying us already, we will own this house, free and clear."

"Wow." Sam was genuinely blown away. "That really is a heck of a deal."

"Yes and thank heavens." Rose nodded. "I have a lot of faith in your sister, but I refuse to spend all of the money earned from her first hit CD, because it may turn out to be her only one. Your futures are too important for us to risk spending all the money Danni is making right now. Without this TV deal, we would have had to choose between a college fund for you and your sister, and this amazing house, which is not only near the stables, but is two blocks away from the best school in town. This way, we were able to get both!"

Sam's jaw dropped. Her mom hadn't forgotten about her. The TV show hadn't come about because her mom was being greedy or thoughtless; Rose was trying to be responsible and ensure that Sam has a great life right now *and* the opportunity to go to college and be whatever she wanted when she grew up.

Rose stirred her tea. "Your old mom may not be the brightest bulb in the chandelier, but I certainly know better than to count my chickens before they've hatched."

"Mom," she said softly, "I believe that is the smartest thing I've ever heard you say."

"Thank you, Sam." Rose glowed, but then she realized what she'd just heard. "I think."

Sam giggled as she hopped up, gave her mom a kiss on the cheek, and ran up to her bedroom.

She ran straight to the mirror and began pounding.

"Come on, Blu!" she yelled. "You have to be in there by now."

Blu's booming voice filled Sam's room. "Apparently you have forgotten that you don't need to yell for me to hear you. Perhaps you didn't understand me fully. When you shout like that, your incredibly loud voice is picked up by one of the many microphones hidden all around; thus, what I end up hearing in my headphones sounds something like this…"

The mirror slid up; Blu stuck his head out of the control, leaned toward Sam, and screamed directly into her ear, "BLAH! BLAH! BLAAAAAH!"

Sam, laughing harder than she had in weeks, stumbled backward and landed on the floor at Blu's feet.

He peered down at her. "Now do you understand?"

Still convulsing with laughter, Sam managed to nod.

Appearing rather pleased that he'd made his point, Blu grinned and returned to his seat inside the control room. Sam picked herself up and followed him.

"Where have you been?" she implored. "I have so much to tell you! You missed a real scene with Danni and Mr. Wannabee last night! I turned around and you were gone."

Blu searched through a stack of videotapes. "I didn't miss a thing. Your mom showed up, so I got out of the way and returned to following your wacky exploits from the safety of my comfy chair here."

Sam furrowed her brow as she tried to understand everything that had happened to her last night. "There's something I still don't get," she said as she scratched her head. "We didn't have the video crew with us at the restaurant, how…" Sam remembered asking Robert how he had known that the family needed help last night and how Michi had told her that Blu had had something to do with it. "Hey, how did you know that we were in trouble at that café? Did you have Michi and Lou secretly trailing us?"

Blu found the tape he'd been searching for and popped it into a VCR. "Guilty as charged."

"Blu!" Sam moaned. "How could you do that?"

Blu sat in his chair and turned to face Sam directly. "Come on now. You know I'm only doing my job. You wanted a quiet family evening, so I told Michi and Lou to hang back, to give you all space. When I saw things escalating, I called Robert and warned him that either he get over to help you out, or I would. I knew he'd step up for the chance to play the hero. I didn't accept this job to become a security guard or a babysitter; I'm just doing my best to make this as painless as possible for everyone involved."

Sam bit her lower lip as she thought about Blu's words. It all seemed to make sense.

"Yeah, okay, I get all that, and I guess that was pretty cool of you."

"You *guess*?" chuckled Blu. "Man-oh-man, you are one tough audience."

"I know that was pretty cool of you," she shot back, "pretty darn cool."

Even though he waved his hand as if to say, "it was nothing," Sam could see that Blu sincerely appreciated her compliment.

Blu reached into the shadows of the control room and grabbed another chair. He slid it over and turned it around so it faced the biggest monitor in the room.

"I don't know what you feel like doing right now, but I think I'm going to sit here and watch the very first episode of *The Devine Life*. You can watch too if you'd like," he teased.

"You are funny," she replied flatly, "very very funny."

Blu beamed a ridiculously large grin at Sam, making her crack up for real. He chortled at his own goofiness as he reached over to play the video.

In the few seconds in-between Blu's hitting the "play" button on the VCR and the moment the show actually began, Sam was overcome with a sick feeling. What was she about to see? Would she look foolish?

Would her family seem shallow or dippy? Sam wrapped her arms around her stomach in the hope of calming it down; she suddenly feared she might throw up all over Blu. She began to feel dizzy, so she closed her eyes, but opened them again when she heard her own voice yelling, "I just want a normal life. A normal house and a normal life!" coming out of the TV screen in front of her.

For the next twenty minutes, Sam watched bits and bites of everything she'd lived through during the past five days. It wasn't as bad as Sam had thought it would be; in fact, it was kind of fun. Blu had clipped together tiny pieces of her family's life in a way that was entertaining, but not insulting. Rose appeared to be a loving, if kind of nutty, mom. Danni seemed to be a sweet young woman who didn't know how to deal with all the attention coming her way. Sam came off as a smart girl who cared more about her family and friends than money or fame. Sam was surprised to find herself enjoying the show.

"This isn't so bad," she said to Blu.

Blu gave her a thumbs up, but stayed silent.

Sam leaned forward when she saw something on

the screen she hadn't been around to notice when it had happened. She was watching something happening in the dining room, the morning of the terrible family meeting. She saw herself walk out of the room while Danni, Rose, and Robert continued to make plans for the trip up to Canada. Rose raised her head and watched Sam exit the dining room; she then turned to Danni and Robert and said, "Listen, you two, this is all very exciting, but we can't forget for a moment that poor Sam wants none of this. If I catch you," she glared at Robert, "either one of you, treating Samantha like she's in the way or any less than an essential part of this family, then so help me, I'll cancel every concert, public appearance, TV show, whatever. I mean it! Family comes first. Do I make myself clear?"

Danni smiled and nodded. "Yup, I hear you, Mom. I'll be more careful."

Robert also nodded, but his voice gave away the fact that he was rather bored with the subject. "Crystal clear, Rose. The kid is important."

Rose's voice was soft, but she drilled into Robert with her eyes. "The *kid* has a name, and I'll thank you to start using it."

The color drained out of Robert's face as he nodded more forcefully. "*Samantha* is important."

"No way!" Sam turned to Blu. "No way!"

"Hang on," he told her. "You're going to love this last part."

Sam studied the screen intently and almost fell out of her chair when she realized what she was now looking at. The screen showed Rose, Danni, Sam, Olga, and Inga standing outside the café last night. The entire scene with the pager thingy and the fat lady yelling at Sam and the attack of the paparazzi played out as if it were a scripted comedy show. Sam couldn't help but laugh.

How strange, she thought, *it didn't seem so entertaining last night, but now as I watch it, it was funny, truly funny!* Plus, having the whole situation on videotape showed that the whole "wait–weight thing" had been a misunderstanding. She now had proof that neither she nor Danni had meant to be mean or to insult that poor lady; it had all been a genuine mistake. Maybe having a camera crew following her around and documenting her life wasn't such a "lose-lose" after all; maybe there was a "win" in

this mess that she hadn't seen before.

Blu reached across to hit the "stop" button as the screen went black. He sat back in his chair without looking at Sam. "All right, you kept your end of the deal. You put up with the crew and me for five days. Now you've seen it. What do you think?"

Sam stood up and began pacing around the control room. This was a big decision.

"Before I give you my answer, I have a few more questions," she said in her most serious tone. "Could you promise to never show really embarrassing stuff, like me barfing or picking my nose?"

Blu had to bite his tongue to stop himself from not laughing at the question. "You think you're the only person who picks her nose? Get real, even the Queen of England goes digging in there sometimes."

Sam walked out of the control room and over to her window sill. She looked out over at the stables and then down at the pool. Robert and Rose were arguing, Danni was floating on a raft while Jean and Jehan were fighting for her attention, each one trying to get Danni to pick their preferred colors of fabrics, and Michi and Lou were trying to videotape all of this without falling into the water. Sam swung her entire body around so she was facing the control room with her arms crossed in front of her. "Would you let me hang out in the control room anytime I want?"

There was a very long pause. When Blu finally did respond, his voice was steely. "You do realize that I could get fired for that."

Sam stuck out her lower lip and made a pouty face, with big, sad, puppy-dog eyes. She batted her lashes directly at the mirror.

Blu tried to keep his voice steely, but now there was a hint of laughter. "That does not work on me. I told you I have four sisters. I am immune."

Sam jumped up and threw her arms in the air. "I'll let you read my blog!"

Blu still wasn't interested. "You mean the blog I've been reading for the past five days? The same blog I can see the internet address of from three different cameras every time you post to it? Come on, if you want to make a deal with me, you'll have to do better than that."

Sam hopped off the sill, paced up and down her room, and thought as hard as she could for something else she could use to deal with Blu, but she came up with nothing. "Help me! I'm trying to make this work. If we do the show, I want to be able to escape my crazy world when things get too intense out here. Please, Blu! There has to be some way we can come to an agreement on this. Please?"

Blu let out a sigh. He stuck his arm out into Sam's room and motioned for Sam to come back over toward the control room.

In a very quiet voice, Blu explained, "Here's the thing. A show like this is only fun if people are real. No faking. No acting. I'll cut out your nose picking and let you visit the control room whenever you want, if…"

Sam waited breathlessly. "IF…?"

"If," Blu continued, "you make sure your family keeps it real. No getting dressed in your Sunday best for breakfast. No using big words you wouldn't normally use. You all have to be your normal selves, the good, the bad, and the embarrassing. You get me?"

"I get you!" Sam then put her hand over her heart and declared, "I, Samantha Sue Devine, solemnly promise you, Mr. Malcolm Bluford, that I will do my absolute best to be plain old me, myself and I at all times and will do everything within my power to get my mom and sister to do the same."

She gave Blu a very formal nod of her head, spun around, and ran to her computer.

So I'm wondering...who is to say how normal one person's reality is compared to somebody else's? Maybe what's normal for us is what works best for us, not what other people try to tell us it should be. Whatever. I'm willing to give my new, kind of weird reality a chance to see if it can start feeling "normal" for me and my family...for a little while, at least.

Sam hit the "send" button to post her blog to the internet. She pulled out a hidden bottle of orange cream soda and took a massive swig, turned back to the mirror, which had been lowered into place, smiled, let out a window-rattling burp, proudly stuck a finger up her nose and gave Blu a big, wet raspberry.

Blu's booming laughter could be heard throughout the entire house. "Classy! Very classy."

Catch up with more of Sam's blogs in her other two ☆ fabulously funny books..

**Join Sam for another
spectacular book in the series...**

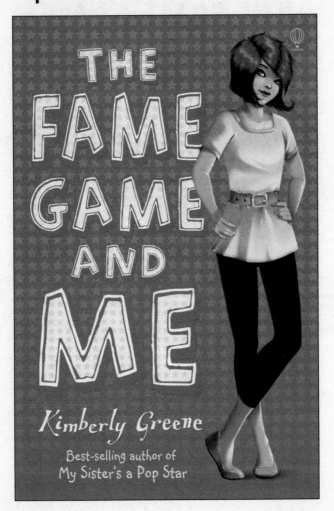

THE FAME GAME AND ME

Kimberly Greene

Best-selling author of
My Sister's a Pop Star

THE FAME GAME AND ME

Hi, I'm Sam, welcome to my blog!

Some people dream of being famous.
Well, I am – and it's a *nightmare*!
My sister Danni is a big-time
POP PRINCESS, so I spend most of
my life trying to figure out the rules
to this freaky FAME GAME!

Danni's discovered it's tough
at the top since a rival pop-diva
started competing for the #1 spot. And
I've just found out an AMAZING secret
about our family. I only hope our life in the
limelight won't make things even
CRAZIER – but I guess that's
showbiz, right?

ISBN: 9780794529000

**Sam gets ready for the cameras
in another thrilling book...**

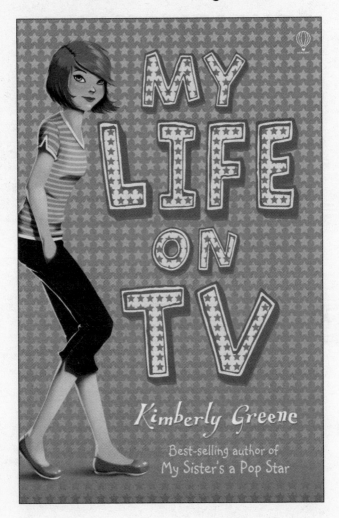

MY
LIFE
ON
TV

Kimberly Greene

Best-selling author of
My Sister's a Pop Star

MY LIFE ON TV

Hi, I'm Sam, welcome to my blog!

Listen up, I'm gonna be starring in my own TV show! Freaky right? Life in the limelight is not for me, but things are kinda strange right now.
My sister's quit being a pop princess so I've got to look after the family. I'm cool with that, but I'm not cool with my co-star. He's pretending to like me for the paparazzi, but it's one great big act.

And guess what – I'm dealing with my first major crush. There's a boy I really want to kiss and when that first kiss happens it just *has* to be special...

ISBN: 9780794529017

☆ A few things you didn't know about ☆ KIMBERLY GREENE ☆

☆ Which five words would you use to describe yourself?

☆ Busy

☆ Chocoholic

☆ Funny

☆ Devilish

☆ Relentless

☆ How do you spend a typical day?

Every day is different, but I always get my morning started by walking down to the local Coffee Bean & Tea Leaf for breakfast with my family and friends.

Once I've finished my beloved Blueberry-Pomegranate Tea Latte (no sugar added – natch!) and got my two-year-old to stop yapping and eat his banana, we head home, stopping only to say hello to EVERY SINGLE human and puppy dog we encounter along the way (sigh). Once we get back home, I'm insanely busy with meetings, doing research, creating presentations, materials and movies for my fellow professors and our graduate students (yup, I'm a teacher – of teachers). I am on my computer at least eight hours a day. I have a special file on my laptop where I keep a running list of future book ideas and I find myself adding all kinds of little thoughts or funny character quirks to it almost everyday. These days, many of my ideas come from stuff my little boy has said or done; having a two-year-old with the vocabulary of a ten-year-old is crazy entertaining!

☆ How do you write?

I think *a lot* before I write. I try to "see" each "scene" of a story in my head and then replay it with small changes to ensure each word that goes into the book is worth reading.

☆ What is your ideal way to spend a day off?
SKIING!!!!!!!!!!!!!!!!!!!!!!!!!!!!!!!!!

If skiing isn't an option (which it isn't very often these days), then any day where I can be with my family, walking along the beach or playing in the backyard, is better than anything.

Although, I do miss riding my motorcycle; I have to find more time for that.

☆ What would you be if you weren't a writer?
I've been writing stories since I was eight years old. Getting my work published has truly been a dream come true, but honestly, even if I hadn't achieved this goal – I'd still be writing.

☆ What's on your iPod?
These days I have mostly movies and photos taking up ALL the space on my iPod. My little boy has given me the opportunity to revisit all kinds of movies and music I loved when I was a kid.